"You should fin[d]
dangerous," Rem remarked.

"What I do is none of your business. What do you need from Ammar?" Haley repeated.

"Why do you do it?"

"Answer me," she insisted.

"Why does someone as fragile as you come to dangerous countries and chase terrorists?" Rem asked.

"Is Ammar a terrorist?"

He just looked at her.

"Is he Hezbollah?" she asked.

"What do you think?"

So Ammar was a Hezbollah terrorist. Nothing surprising there. "I'm not fragile," she told him.

He pushed his chair back and stood. Moving with deliberate slowness, he came to stand beside her chair. She strained her neck to look up at him.

"No?" He reached to brush some hair behind her shoulder.

Haley tensed. Her heart flew.

Dear Reader,

Cullen McQueen's secret counterterror organization, TES, is bigger and stronger than ever in the third installment of the ALL McQUEEN'S MEN miniseries, *Unmasking the Mercenary.*

I was after something a little different with this one. I wanted a strong heroine with a dark past to capture the heart of Rem D'Evereux, Mr. Badness incarnate. With a rough childhood that led him down the wrong path for too many years, he has trouble connecting with his heroic side. But then he meets Haley Engen, an ex-POW who's determined to win the battle against her own inner demons. The two have a common bond and make each other grow.

Writing Rem as a dark and dangerous hero with a seriously questionable résumé—while still retaining his heroism—was a challenge. But it was a rewarding one. He isn't TES material. But he could be. When bad is really good, a little dose of Nietzsche goes nicely with a love story like this one. I hope you agree!

Jennifer

JENNIFER MOREY

Unmasking the Mercenary

ROMANTIC
SUSPENSE

 **SILHOUETTE BOOKS**

Recycling programs for this product may not exist in your area.

ISBN-13: 978-0-373-27676-9

UNMASKING THE MERCENARY

Copyright © 2010 by Jennifer Morey

This edition published by arrangement with Harlequin Books S.A.

For questions and comments about the quality of this book please contact us at Customer_eCare@Harlequin.ca.

® and TM are trademarks of Harlequin Books S.A., used under license. Trademarks indicated with ® are registered in the United States Patent and Trademark Office, the Canadian Trade Marks Office and in other countries.

Visit Silhouette Books at www.eHarlequin.com

Printed in U.S.A.

Books by Jennifer Morey

Silhouette Romantic Suspense

★*The Secret Soldier* #1526
★*Heiress Under Fire* #1578
Blackout at Christmas #1583
  "Kiss Me on Christmas"
★*Unmasking the Mercenary* #1606

★All McQueen's Men

JENNIFER MOREY

has been dreaming up stories since she fell in love with *The Black Stallion* by Walter Farley. With a BS in geology from Colorado State University, she is associate project manager for the spacecraft segment of a satellite imagery and information company. She has received several awards for her writing—one that led to the publication of her debut novel, *The Secret Soldier*—and she is a 2009 two-time RITA® Award nominee and Best First Book Golden Quill winner. She lives in Denver, Colorado, with her new man and their pet store: three dogs— Maddie, Dug and Booger—and plenty of fish. She loves to hear from readers. You can visit her Web site at www.jennifermorey.com.

To Buddy Mizner, for never giving up on me while I dated less deserving men, and for making me write when all I wanted to do was be with him.
May I always "wreck you." I'm all yours.

As always, to my family and friends, and my critique partners—Susan LeDoux, Laura Leonard, Sandra Kerns, Annette Elton and Julie Stevens.

And to Mom.

Wish she was here to see this!

Chapter 1

"You getting this?"

Haley Engen looked up from the intel file to see the monitor on her laptop computer. Her partner, Travis Todd, had a video camera disguised as a button on his shirt. It had audio capability, but he hadn't spoken to her until now. The camera focused on the forty-something Lebanese man who ran a market on United Nations Drive. He was arguing with someone she didn't recognize. Standing behind his checkout counter, the Lebanese glanced around the four-aisle market as though worried he'd be heard. He passed over Travis without any sign of suspicion and then turned back to the stranger. For as big as Travis was, he could blend in when he tried. Right now he was fingering a candy bar.

"Yeah," she said. "Who is that he's talking to?"

"Never seen him before," he answered in a low voice. He never talked during surveillance, but the stranger presented a possible new twist to the mission.

They'd been tracking the Lebanese man in Monrovia, Liberia, for a few days now, watching his daily routine. The file in front of her said he was a diamond merchant named Habib Maalouf who had family history with Hezbollah. That made him worth a closer look. Which was the reason for this little endeavor into the fine, forsaken land of extortionists and murdering rebels. Diamonds didn't wash through the country the way they did in Sierra Leone, but it was filled with people who'd do anything to get their hands on them.

"I'll send something to Odie and see what she can come up with." She cropped a picture of the man who'd resumed his heated discussion with the Lebanese merchant. Too bad they hadn't bugged the checkout counter.

Travis passed the front counter and the two men stopped talking. Then the monitor filled with passing cars and people walking along the street.

Haley spotted a man leaning his shoulder against the white wall of a hat vendor across the street. His height and size made her notice him. He was very tall and big. Not overly muscle-bound, but solid and strong. Broad shoulders filled his white T-shirt. Round biceps. Sinewy forearms. Thick black hair and dark stubble. The way he perused the activity on the street gave her a chill. He gave nothing away. Didn't smile. Didn't alter his expression. Just watched. His gaze landed on Travis and then moved on.

Haley still-framed the digital recording and cropped another picture. She couldn't explain why, but the guy gave her a funny feeling.

Travis left the busy activity along United Nations Drive. No one appeared ahead of him.

"You heading back?" She didn't want to alert Travis to the man. Certain men scared her, and this one was no exception. He had a rugged, hard look that intimidated her. Maybe it was the lack of emotion that got to her. It reminded her of the way the Iraqi insurgents who'd captured her five years ago had looked at her. She couldn't expunge it from her memory any more than she could overcome the lasting effect of her ordeal.

"Yeah. I'm hot and sweaty and hungry."

"Yeah?" She smiled. "So where do you want to risk food poisoning tonight?"

He chuckled. "Let's stick with seafood."

"Agreed. I'm never going to want to eat meat here again."

She pasted an image of the man with the merchant into an e-mail message and typed a quick note to Odelia Frank. The Army operations captain was the glue that held Tactical Executive Security together, and the reason many of their counterterror missions were so successful. Haley didn't send her the image of the man outside the hat shop.

"See you in two."

"Over and out." She pulled off the headpiece to her radio. By the time her laptop shut down, Travis came through the door of their bland hotel room. At least it was clean.

He'd insisted on one room with two beds. He always did that. Overprotected her on TES missions. Sometimes she appreciated it, but only when she felt weaker than usual. Which, since Iraq, she occasionally did.

"We'll need to keep an eye on that man our merchant met today. You think that button will look good on one of my blouses?"

"Are you suggesting you should do the ops next time?"

He knew she was, and that sparked her ire. She kept it in check. "They might recognize you."

"You're the comms and intel specialist. It's what Cullen hired you for."

"I can do more than that and you know it. I have training."

"If we need a closer look, we'll rely on Odie and get it electronically from her files."

"Don't do that, Travis." There he went again, overprotecting her.

"I'm not arguing, Haley. If you don't want to do this my way, you'll have to take it up with the boss."

"He'll only say what you ask him to say." Cullen McQueen was one of the toughest men she'd ever met, but when it came to women, he didn't budge on safety factors.

"It isn't my fault he agrees with me. And he's only watching out for you."

"Why? Because I'm a woman?" She told him what she thought of that in French.

"Stop that," he said.

He didn't like it when she spoke in French because he didn't know what she was saying.

"What did you say?" he asked.

"Nothing."

"You always do that when you get mad."

That wasn't the only time. She'd learned French at a young age and it came in handy at times.

"What did you say?" he demanded this time.

"I said you men are all the same."

"Haley, you know I wouldn't want anyone else on the other end of my radio. You're the brains of every operation."

She got up from the hard wood chair and walked over to him. "Flattery doesn't work on me. Haven't you figured that out by now?"

"Why are you always so eager to put yourself in danger?"

That took her aback. "I'm not."

His mouth curved into a doubtful frown.

"I just want to make a difference," she said, wondering if she sounded defensive.

He didn't comment further. He didn't have to. And she was glad he didn't press the issue. Everyone at TES knew about her capture. She'd never admit how much the possibility of remembering everything scared her. She didn't know what happened after the insurgents started beating her, and she never wanted to. But she did remember the special forces soldiers who came to rescue her. Joining TES had given her the closest thing to retribution she could find. It was her way of fighting back, something she hadn't been able to do when the insurgents had attacked her.

"I can't think of you as one of the guys," Travis said, "so don't ask me to."

She rose up onto her toes and pressed a kiss to his cheek. "You're like a brother to me."

He smiled but didn't say anything, softness still in his eyes. When she'd first met him, he'd intimidated her the same way the man outside the hat shop had. Once she got to know him, though, she wasn't afraid anymore. They'd grown closer and had become friends.

They'd come close to more once, but she didn't feel that kind of chemistry with him. That was why she hadn't had a relationship with him—which would have been the first since her attack. Even if she were physically attracted to him, the idea of sleeping with him made her wince sometimes. He wasn't an unattractive man, he was just, well, big. And always so careful around her. Like he might break her if he touched her. So he did all he felt he could do. Protect her.

If she couldn't be intimate with someone as gentle and considerate as Travis, despite his looming appearance, would she be able to be intimate with any man? Iraq had changed her. The doctors had told her plenty. More than she wanted to know. Not having a memory of the torture didn't erase the fact that it had happened. That was the part that bothered her most. She didn't know what would have been worse, knowing how her body had been abused from a medical perspective or remembering it in vivid detail.

"Come on." Travis headed for the door. "Let's drive over to Broad Street. There's a place I know that has good seafood."

She picked up her Walther P99 Quick Action 9 mm pistol

and tucked it in her belt holster, covering it with her short-sleeved white T-shirt. Like Travis, she wore jeans.

Travis led her out of the room and down the stairs leading to the Mamba Point Hotel lobby. If one could call it a lobby. It looked more like the entrance to an office building, which was what it had once been. Crossing the dark wood floor, she followed Travis outside. A large gravel parking area was enclosed by an eight-foot white cement wall. They got into a Jeep the hotel had retrieved for them and drove to the solid iron gate at the entrance of the parking area. The guard opened the gate and Haley waved as they passed.

Travis drove to United Nations Drive and made a left onto Newport. The Jeep was open, and the wind messed the tendrils of hair that had loosened from her ponytail. When they reached Broad, Travis turned right. Wondering why he passed the restaurant, she saw him glance at the rearview mirror and apprehension reared up in her.

"What's the matter?" she asked.

"We're being followed."

Her heart jumped into an alarmed rhythm. She twisted on the seat and saw a beat-up blue SUV filled with several men. How had this happened? She didn't understand. Travis was always so careful.

"You couldn't have been followed to the market," she said.

"I know."

He was thinking what she was thinking; someone else had been keeping watch outside the market. Had that someone seen him watching the market owner?

Haley remembered the man outside the hat shop and wondered if she'd made a calculated error not telling Travis. Her judgment may have been clouded by her reaction. Did the man work for the stranger who'd met the market owner? Without more to go on it was hard to tell. She and Travis were here only to gather information. It was just the two of them. But somehow they'd been discovered.

Travis pounded the steering wheel once with his palms and swore. Stepping on the gas, he skidded into a right turn. Battered buildings whizzed past them.

Gunfire exploded. Travis swerved when the back tires gave. The men chasing them were aiming for the tires.

Haley fought the horribly familiar rush of fear and dread. She closed her eyes against memory, then pulled her P99 from her waist holster and twisted in the seat to fire back at the SUV.

Travis turned onto Benson. The U.S. embassy was too far away. As he turned onto Lynch, more gunfire rang. The front left tire blew and Travis couldn't hold the Jeep. They spun and jerked to a halt.

Haley scrambled out of the Jeep. She aimed over the hood of the vehicle as gunshots splattered the other side of it.

"Travis!" she screamed and fired her gun over and over, trying to cover him.

She heard him moan a swear word.

"Oh, God."

Dark-skinned rebels holding automatic rifles emerged from the other side of the SUV. She registered other things, dirty clothes, unkempt hair, very little muscle-weight, but kept her mind on defending Travis. She reached into the Jeep and yanked open the glove box for another clip. Reloading, she crouched with her back against the Jeep door. Seeing a hand stretching past the front of the Jeep, she realized Travis had crawled there, but now he wasn't moving. With the angle of the Jeep, he was safe, for now at least.

Rolling so she could fire over the hood of the Jeep, she saw the men were drawing closer. She took careful aim and fired. She got two of them before she had to duck. There were four left.

Crawling toward Travis, she came around the front of the Jeep. She didn't have time to check for his pulse. Rising slowly, she fired again. They were so close. One. Two. But she only got the second man's arm. She ducked again as they fired back, then rose to continue shooting. She ran out of bullets.

The first dark-skinned man approached the front of the Jeep. He was thin and wore a dirty tan shirt that hung to the thighs of his equally dirty jeans. The second went around the back of the Jeep. He was shorter but just as thin. The third followed him, just a young boy, maybe thirteen. Sick fear gave a stark beat to her pulse. She fought it. They weren't big men. She might be able to overpower them. She'd become a good fighter since Iraq.

Still holding her gun, she moved away from Travis as the three surrounded her. She turned, keeping them in sight. The tallest one wore a leer she would have loved to blast off his face with a bullet. There was an ugly space between his two big front teeth. The one she'd injured said something in his native tongue, something angry. The young boy looked around, keeping watch for any interference. But what people had been on the street had fled with the first round of gunfire.

"You will come with us," the gap-toothed man said in a rolling West African accent.

She said nothing, just kept backing away.

The gap-toothed man walked faster toward her. Instead of running as she was sure he expected, she waited for him to get close enough. Then she angled her leg for a kick, catching him on the chest and throwing him off balance. He stumbled backward. She whacked him high on the back of his neck with her P99. He dropped to the ground unconscious.

The one she'd injured pushed the barrel of his rifle to the side of her head. She had no choice other than to go still. If she moved at all, would he kill her?

At least she'd die fighting.

"You come quiet or we kill you now," he said.

The insurgents had told her that in Iraq, too. Back then, she'd gone. This time…

Two moves, one with her hand slamming the barrel of the rifle upward, the other driving her elbow back to give his solar plexus a good jab, were enough to distract him. A shot rang out but she didn't pause. She pivoted just enough and drove a hard kick to the man's groin. He dropped in agony. Not so tough after all. Skinny bastard.

She went for his gun, but before she reached it, the kid appeared in her peripheral vision, raising his rifle and hitting her with the end of the handle hard on the back of her head. She lost coherency for a minute. Blinking, she realized she was sprawled on the ground. She rolled onto her butt, unable to focus very well. She searched the ground for a gun. One lay a few feet from the man she'd kicked in the groin, who still squirmed in pain. The other lay near the gap-toothed man's unconscious body, but he was farther away.

The kid gripped her arm and started to pull her to her feet. A sound made him let go and straighten, turning to look toward the Jeep.

Haley blinked more and cleared her vision enough to see a huge man striding toward them, aiming a pistol.

"Get away from her," he said.

His deadly tone and ground-eating strides should have been enough to deter any man less than half his size. And then it dawned on her who he was. The man who'd stood outside the hat shop. Was he going to help her?

The kid let go of her arm and aimed his rifle.

The man from the hat shop fired once. Yelping, the kid dropped the rifle with a clatter, holding his arm as he fell onto his backside.

Movement to her right made her look there. The man she'd kicked in the groin was trying to crawl toward his gun. His hand curled around the handle and he rolled onto his backside. Another gunshot stilled him. The hat shop man had shot him in the chest.

She reached for the fallen rifle the same time the kid went for it. He yanked it from her grasping hands just before the hat shop man swung his meaty fist, smashing against the boy's head. The kid fell back and didn't move, unconscious. She wouldn't have been able to kill a teenager, either, although it wasn't uncommon to see Liberia's youth among the corrupted.

Head still spinning, Haley once again reached for the rifle. But the hat shop man picked it up and straightened, looking down at her with that same impassive expression that had chilled her when she'd first seen him. Then he searched their surroundings, propping the barrel of the rifle on his hulking shoulder while eyes shadowed by an ominous brow missed nothing. Apparently satisfied that the volley of gunfire had scared off anything with a pulse, he turned and went to the Jeep. Haley held her breath while he knelt beside Travis and checked for breath and then a heartbeat.

Travis.

Oh, God, please let him live.

The big man pulled a knife from a pocket on his pant leg and cut Travis's T-shirt down the front. Then he ripped a strip of it away, pushing some of it into the gunshot wound he'd exposed to help stop the bleeding. He was unemotional and methodical. When he finished, he stood and stepped toward her with those long, smooth strides that showed his intimidating strength. He was not afraid of anything. His body language shouted it. There was a darkness about him, hanging all around him and setting her on edge.

When he knelt in front of her, she had to stifle an audible sound of alarm. Thick black hair accentuated his terrifying light blue eyes. So much power there.

"Is he okay?" she asked.

"We need to get him to a doctor. I know one that's less than five minutes from here. Can you walk?"

She started to climb to her feet. He helped her, but she pulled her arm free of his grip, stumbling back as her head swam. He appeared to want to help her and Travis, but trust was difficult for her even under normal circumstances. She shoved away his reaching hand and started toward Travis. The motion made her head swim. Nausea gathered and pooled.

Not now.

She lost her balance and began to fall. No. She was going to pass out. The hat shop man's arm against her back stopped her, and the last thing she registered was him lifting her.

Rem D'Evereux put the woman in the passenger's seat of his SUV and went to get her partner. He carried the man to the backseat and deposited him there. He wasn't a light man, so the task wasn't graceful. Hurrying around to the driver's side, Rem sat behind the wheel and glanced over at the woman as he started the SUV. She had to be an operative just like her partner. He tried not to let her beauty make that hard for him to absorb, but it was.

Why were they watching Habib? Who had sent them? And why?

He didn't think they knew about Ammar Farid Salloum. Rem had been following the man for a week now and hadn't noticed any indicators anyone else was doing the same. It had taken him a while to catch up to him. He still couldn't believe how blind he'd been. He should have been able to predict Ammar's motives, but grief and anger had interfered. Now it made him dream of seeing the man gutted and served to the cannibal rebels of Monrovia, men who ate their enemies for spiritual strength.

Had two American operatives gotten a whiff of the same

foul scent? Were they working for the U.S. government or someone else? If he had to guess, it was the former. How much did they know? Was it Habib they were interested in? And if so, why? It made Rem uncomfortable. He couldn't have anyone learning too much about his reasons for tailing Ammar. Especially any special forces types.

He looked over at the woman again. Her partner was seen leaving the market, and that man had followed him to the Mamba Point Hotel. Rem had lagged far enough behind to stay inconspicuous. He'd watched along with the other man as the woman's partner reemerged from the hotel with her. Her beauty arrested him. There was something odd about her. She strangled her long, dark hair in a ponytail and wore jeans and a T-shirt as if she wanted to pass as a man. He'd like to be the one to let her know there wasn't a chance in an all-male hell of that. Not only was she beautiful, there was an air of fragility about her. And that was what had struck him as odd. What was a woman like her doing snooping around in a cesspool like Monrovia?

It was one of the first questions he'd ask her when she regained consciousness. Had someone with the U.S. government caught on to what Rem already knew? It grated his nerves the same as it made him want to smile.

Ammar thought he was untouchable. Over the last week, Rem had wiped the smirk off that worthless terrorist's face by turning up when least expected, hovering, watching. Always a threat—an unpredictable one. More than once, Rem could have killed him, but he hadn't. And Ammar knew it. Everything had been going according to plan.

Until the two American operatives showed up.

He'd never been any good at prying information from women. He couldn't hurt them the way he could hurt men. But the one next to him might know something important. Tall and slender, she had the deepest blue eyes he'd ever seen, and that long, dark chocolate hair would look so much better out of the ponytail. His desire to see it that way made him uncomfortable. Why was he so interested in a do-gooder like her?

He drove to a stop in front of Essam Haddad's shack of a home that doubled as a clinic. Reddish dirt and gravel surrounded the one-story building packed among a hodgepodge of other shacks. The only thing adorning the front yard was a step leading to the front door.

Rem left the woman and hefted the man from the backseat and carried him to the door, leaving a trail of dropped blood. Essam opened the door and spoke rapidly in his native tongue, helping Rem carry the big man inside. Through the front room, they entered a one-room clinic. It didn't look like much, but if Rem were ever in need of lifesaving treatment, he'd trust Essam over any other place offering medical treatment in this country.

With the man on one of two clinic beds, Rem turned and went to retrieve the woman. Essam looked up from his busy hands and shook his head as Rem came back into the clinic and deposited the woman on the other narrow bed.

"You should quit your foolishness, Rem. How many more of these will I have to patch up before you're the one brought to me bleeding?" He swept his bloodied glove over his patient before resuming his work. "You will end up like this." He'd already inserted an IV and was now digging around in his patient's wounds.

"I don't know who these people are. I think they came to check out Habib Maalouf and someone didn't like it, as you can see." He nodded down at the shot-up man.

Essam didn't look up from his work. "Yes, but you were there. One of these times Ammar will be ready for you and then what, hmm?"

"I won't be easy to kill."

"So you think."

"Then I'll have died trying to do something right." And that would be a first, which had a certain appeal he'd never admit to anyone.

"You are willing to die for this cause?"

Without question. But he kept the thought to himself.

"You blame yourself too much. It is what drives you."

"I don't confuse the truth with blame." He'd learned that the hard way. He'd also learned how to be hard to kill. Nobody learned survival like a fourteen-year-old working the streets.

Now Essam looked up. "You should go home and get an honest job. Put your past behind you, Rem. It is the only way you will ever find happiness for your black heart."

"There are no honest jobs for me." It was too late for that. He'd lie and cheat all the way to hell if it gave him Farid Abi Salloum's head.

"You've made some bad decisions, I will agree, but it is never too late to change. It is your hatred that will get you killed if you don't."

Bad decisions. Rem had to smother a derisive grunt. He'd survived, that's all. But that survival had led him down a dark and dangerous path, and now there was only one way off.

"Once Farid is dead, I'll bury my hatred with him. You have my word."

Essam shook his head. "You are a better man than you realize."

Rem didn't comment. Essam had said as much before, but he didn't know the full extent of Rem's past. He knew only the part that had driven Rem here. Better or worse, it didn't matter to Rem. He was who he was and there was no changing that.

"When have you acted out of cruelty?" Essam asked. "Never once. Even at your lowest, you have not betrayed your morals. I do not have to know more than I do to be sure of this. You are not a man who can be bought. You are not a man who turns his back on the helpless. You are not a man who confuses right from wrong. You may think it is your failures that have cost you so much, but what you do not see is that it was your honor instead."

His honor had cost him? He had no honor, so how was that possible? "You're a good friend, Essam. I'll always remember that."

"Pah!" Essam swatted his hand in dismissal.

Rem backed to the only chair in the room and kept quiet. At last the doctor finished with the shot-up man and moved over to the woman.

"Is he going to live?" Rem asked.

"I do not know. He has lost a lot of blood and I have none to give him."

Essam turned the woman's head and cleaned a gash there. When he stitched the wound, he removed his second pair of gloves and faced Rem. "I have given her a strong pain medication. She may sleep for a while. I will see that they both make it out of Liberia. There is no point in you staying any longer. You did right to bring them here."

"The woman stays with me."

"Rem—"

"I need her."

"She'll be safer outside this country."

"She stays with me. At least until I've had a chance to question her. After that, I'll make sure she gets to the United States unharmed."

"Where will you take her until then?"

"Somewhere safe."

"As long as she is with you, she will never be safe."

Chapter 2

Haley opened her eyes and winced with the steady thud piercing her skull. She blinked her vision clear. Above her, a colorful mural spread over the recessed and elegantly trimmed ceiling. She rolled her head to see the rest of her surroundings. The room was richly appointed. She lay on a queen-sized bed with an off-white quilt. Across from the foot of the bed was an ornately carved armoire. A chair was angled beside it. Through a balcony door to her right, she could see the ocean in the distance.

Where was she?

This couldn't be Monrovia.

Sitting up, she put her hand on her head when the thudding boomed stronger with each heartbeat. She pushed the covers aside and slid off the bed to stand. The cool, taupe-colored tile chilled her feet until she stepped onto a dark blue rug. She was wearing the same clothes she'd worn when she and Travis were on their way to dinner.

Then it all came crashing upon her. Travis. The hat shop man.

Her pulse fired into frantic beats. She tried to calm her fear. It would only hinder her ability to escape.

She searched the room for her gun. Not seeing it, she went to the armoire and opened the center door. Television. She opened the left side of the armoire. Her duffel bag was on the bottom shelf. She opened it and rooted through her things. No gun. She opened the first drawer below the television. Nothing.

Who had brought her things here? And where the hell was her gun?

She hurried to the door, swung it open, and walked faster than her head could bear. Passing a bathroom and a second bedroom, she slowed her pace when the hall opened to a landing area. A banister and stairway led to the lower level, where she could see the entry and living room and kitchen. Color greeted her everywhere. Through high windows to her left, she could see a tall, thick cement wall and an iron gate with a guard shack. Coiled barbed wire topped the wall.

Still in Monrovia.

Not surprising, she supposed, though the fence made her more than a little nervous. Sliding her hand along the banister, she stepped down the stairs, marveling at the grandeur around her. The villa was silent. On the lower level, she saw two open doors, one another bathroom, the other another bedroom. A third door was shut. It wasn't a huge villa, but it was stunning. Diabolical in a country like Liberia, but she had heard there were some upscale estates near the embassy compounds.

Across pale tile flooring, beautiful French doors stained a rich brown led to a patio. She could see part of a pool, and a pair of male feet lounging on a chair. She opened the door and stepped outside.

The man who'd stopped her attackers lay there, the light covering of dark hair on his muscular chest damp and his smooth, tan skin shining with sweat. She took in the ripples of his abdomen all the way to the waist of the black swim trunks he wore. Beneath the material of the trunks, his thighs were slabs of lean muscle, and the bulge of his calves gave further evidence of his fitness.

Having to remind herself this was not a man she could trust, at least not yet, she looked at his face. His dark sunglasses kept her from knowing if he saw her.

"How are you?" he asked.

Now she knew. "Where is Travis?"

His abdomen bunched as he sat forward and rose to his feet in one continuous movement. She took a step back as he came to a stop in front of her, lifting his sunglasses to prop them on top of his head. The impact of those pale blue eyes both riveted and disconcerted her.

"Still with the doctor," he said.

"Where is he? Is he all right?"

He didn't say anything, and that only increased her apprehension. She was afraid to ask. "Is he going to die?"

"I don't know. He was in pretty bad shape when I left him."

Tears burned her eyes and she covered her mouth to the sound of her gasp.

His expression remained unmoved.

Did the man have no heart? "Where is he? Where did you take him? And why am I here and not with him?" Was he holding her against her will? She tried to control her quivering lower lip and the tears that threatened the fighter in her. *Oh, Travis...you can't die.*

"I can't let you go see him."

"What? Why not?" Had this man kidnapped her? The magnitude of trouble she might be in descended on her full force. What did he know that she didn't? What did he think she knew? She took a few more steps backward. "Who the hell are you?"

He reached out and gently grasped her arm, stopping her withdrawal. "My name is Rem D'Evereux. If I hadn't interrupted your encounter with those rebels, you'd both be dead by now. Travis before you."

Yanking her arm free, she forced herself to remain calm. The bulk of him and the indomitable energy streaming from his icy blue eyes warned her this was not a man to cross. Whatever he wanted from her, she had to be careful.

"Why are you here?" she asked. "Why were you outside the hat shop?"

"I could ask you the same question," he countered.

She decided not to respond.

His gaze roamed all over her face before drilling her with steadiness that unnerved her. "I knew you were just recon the minute I saw you. But what is it you want to know? What brought you here?"

"You saw me?" She ignored his other questions. How long had he been tailing her and Travis? And why hadn't they noticed? "When?"

"Are you government?" he asked instead of acknowledging her.

"Answer my question first."

"I followed Travis from the market."

"He would have noticed someone like you following him."

"Probably, but one of Ammar's guards was ahead of me. I stayed far enough behind to remain out of Travis's sight."

"Ammar?"

"Ammar Farid Salloum."

Was he the one talking to Habib in the market? Yes, it was the man in the picture she'd sent Odie. It had to be. "What do you mean his guard followed Travis? Why would he do that?"

"He saw Travis go into the market after Ammar. Travis didn't know the guard was with Ammar."

"Travis didn't know who Ammar was until he saw him talking to Habib."

"Yes, but to the guard, it looked like he followed Ammar into the market. The guard got suspicious and went in after him and must have seen him watching Habib and Ammar."

"And the guard followed Travis to the hotel."

Rem nodded.

Haley absorbed that a moment. The guard who'd followed must have blended in with anyone else on the street. He hadn't triggered Travis's suspicion. It explained a lot. Then she realized how much Rem had pieced together.

She focused on him. Had he seen the picture she'd taken of him? Recalling her things in the armoire upstairs, she didn't doubt it. He probably had her laptop, too. Quickly, she went through an inventory of what he might have discovered. The e-mail to Odie. Information on Habib. Nothing more. She kept her computer clean most the time.

The picture of him…

"Who are you?" she asked, not wanting to dwell on what he thought of her taking pictures of him.

"I told you, my name is Rem D'Evereux."

"And I'm Haley Engen. Now tell me who you are."

That pushed his mouth into a one-sided grin. "Where did you learn how to fight the way you do?"

She folded her arms and stuck out a foot, angling her head in a silent but clear message.

His grin spread, but never materialized into a full smile. No real humor in it, just an amused and cynical recognition of her tenacity.

"Ammar is a Hezbollah radical with whom I have unfinished business. Apparently you and I have something in common."

Yep, he'd been all over her computer. "Are you government?"

"I believe it's your turn to answer that question for me."

She smiled much the way he had. "No."

"Not government? Then who sent you?"

She cocked her head.

He chuckled, but again, it was cynical, not real humor. "No."

Not government. She didn't think so. He had too many rough edges. Or maybe *reckless* was a better word. Cocky, even, in a quiet, deadly sort of way.

"Who sent you?" he repeated.

No more playing around. She couldn't answer his question and that was that. She kept her face blank.

Any trace of a smile left his face as he studied her, taking his time. "Who is O-324?"

That was Odie's e-mail address, and quite untraceable. "Take me to Travis."

Nothing changed on his face. He remained immovable.

"You can't keep me prisoner here," she said.

"We aren't going anywhere until you tell me everything you know."

He did think she knew something. "About Ammar Farid Salloum? I've never heard of him."

"That I believe, but who were you watching?"

She was afraid to answer him.

"Habib?"

If she told him everything she knew about Habib, what then? She couldn't ignore the feeling he had his own agenda and it might not mesh with hers.

"Why Habib?" he asked in her silence.

She didn't respond. She couldn't trust him.

He blinked, giving away his recognition of her refusal to talk any more on the subject. "You have no idea what you've gotten yourself into."

"Tell me where Travis is."

"He should be on his way to a hospital in Europe by now."

"Which one?"

"I didn't ask."

She stared at him, wondering why he'd gone out of his way to help Travis, yet had brought her here. He could have left Travis to die, but he hadn't. The nobility of the act went against the way his taking her against her will made her feel.

"Why are you doing this?" she finally asked.

He only met her gaze. If she wasn't going to talk, neither was he. That was the message she got. He didn't have to say it for her to know.

Haley glanced at the pool and back at the well-maintained villa. Surveying the perimeter, she followed the jagged edge of the barbed wire and the wall that closed her off from freedom.

"You don't have to worry. You're safe here."

She turned back to him, wary of believing him. "From you?"

The flash of displeasure in his eyes told her he didn't like her question. Without answering, he headed for the door leading into the villa. There, he paused and turned.

"Make yourself at home," he said, and then disappeared inside.

Haley rubbed her arms and once again looked at what she could see of the perimeter wall, wondering if the answer to her question would have been no.

Haley hissed a curse and slammed the armoire door shut. After resting the remainder of the day, her head felt better now. It was hard to believe a day had passed since she and Travis were attacked. She was ready to get out of here, but she still hadn't found her gun. She needed her laptop, too. And the satellite phone that had been in her duffel bag until Rem had gotten hold of it.

She looked once again at the phone on the table beside the bed. The sun had set, and the bedside lamp was the only thing lighting the room. Had he left the phone there deliberately? Did it matter? If she could get a call through to Odie, maybe someone could help her.

She went there and lifted the hand piece. She hesitated before pressing the international number. Rem wouldn't be able to trace the call if she kept it brief. He wouldn't be able to trace it at all if she knew Odie well enough.

She entered the number. Odie answered.

"I can't talk long."

"Haley, my God, where the hell are you two? What happened?"

"Listen carefully. I'm still in Monrovia at a villa along the shore. I'm being held here against my will, but I'm okay."

"You've been kidnapped?"

"Travis has been shot." She told her about the rebels and the man who'd saved her and taken Travis to a doctor. "He's being transported to a hospital in Europe."

Odie cursed a row of curses. "I knew it. Cullen should have never let you go there. Travis was probably so busy watching your back that he forgot to watch his own!"

It hurt that Odie doubted her ability, but she knew the tough woman didn't blame her for Travis getting shot. Still, it got to her that even Odie, a woman, thought Haley didn't belong in an operative role.

"Would you rather I never leave Roaring Creek?" she couldn't help asking. "Like you?"

"Where is Travis, Haley?"

That instantly checked her emotion. Now was no time to let her ego compromise her. "I don't know. And I don't have time to explain. Get me whatever you can on Rem D'Evereux. If I can, I'll call again tomorrow."

She hung up and stared down at her hand on the phone. Letting her breath go, she turned—and sucked it back in.

Rem stood in the now-open doorway, calculation emanating from his impossibly blue eyes. She'd done exactly as he'd predicted.

"Dinner will be ready in a few minutes," he said, and turned. She walked to the doorway and saw him going down the stairs. She followed. Dinner? She could smell something cooking. He cooked?

Downstairs, she didn't see him. Two plates were stacked on the kitchen counter beside two forks. There were two wine glasses, too, and a bottle of red wine. They were unceremoniously placed, just a prep for dinner, but the everyday appeal struck her as odd given her situation. And the man.

She turned and saw a light on in one of the rooms off the living room. The one that had been closed earlier. She went there and stopped in the opening.

Rem looked over his shoulder, the computer illuminated in front of him. On the screen she could see an Internet page. From here it looked like he'd found an article.

"Roaring Creek, Colorado?"

She moved her gaze to him. "How did you...?" She looked back at the computer screen. Then it dawned on her. He'd listened to her conversation with Odie. She'd let her emotion get in the way and had revealed a telling piece of information.

"Want to tell me what's in Roaring Creek or are you going to make me keep surfing?"

"You won't find anything." But wavering confidence made her step farther into the room. Standing behind him, she watched him click on links that pointed to things about the small mountain town.

"Is this where you live?" he asked.

She didn't answer.

He clicked on an old news story about Cullen McQueen and Sabine O'Clery. Haley gritted her teeth as he read about the ex-Delta soldier who'd rescued Sabine from Afghanistan, and, even more damaging, about the exposure of his supersecret company after someone attacked Sabine at her Roaring Creek, Colorado, bookstore.

Before he finished reading, Haley pivoted and marched out of the room. At the kitchen counter, she lifted the bottle of wine and a corkscrew next to it, more for something to do while her mind spun with implication. She finished uncorking the bottle when Rem emerged, his eyes far less threatening now. In fact, he looked a little smug.

She poured wine into one glass and put the bottle down. He stopped beside her and lifted the bottle, pouring wine into his own glass. She turned her back and peered through the window at the dimly lit pool.

"So you're into counterterror operations, is that it? Ex-Delta soldier…supersecret company…it doesn't take much of a leap." She slid her gaze to him when he spoke. He'd put his glass down and went to the oven, removing a pan of lasagna. He put it on a hot pad beside the plates. Next, he went to the refrigerator and removed a bowl of salad. Setting that down, he extended her a plate.

The idea of a man like him cooking was almost comical. Taking the plate, she dished a small amount of food.

"Lasagna?" She couldn't resist the teasing tone that made its way into her voice.

"A guy has to eat."

"Frozen pizza seems more appropriate."

"All out."

She smiled a little and went to sit at the table. Rem sat across from her. She picked at her food, waiting for him to start in again. Because, of course, he would.

"I take it Cullen McQueen restructured his secret company," Rem said. "Who is he working for?"

As if she'd ever tell him. She didn't know, anyway.

"I'm surprised a thug like you can cook," she commented.

He didn't look happy with her moniker.

She cut a bite with her fork and ate a sample. Her brow rose when the flavor burst in her mouth. "Mmm. Good." She ate another bite.

"Why were you casing Habib Maalouf?" Rem asked. He hadn't touched his food yet.

Haley leaned back in her chair with her wineglass and sipped, eyeing him over the rim. "You won't find that on the Internet."

"What clued you to check into Habib?" He sounded more demanding now.

"What clued *you?*"

"If you answer my question, I'll answer yours."

So they were back to that. "What will you do once I tell you?"

"What do you think I'd do?" he countered.

She put her wineglass down and stared at him. He wasn't going to give an inch. She had no doubt he'd used violence to his advantage in the past. It surrounded him, his aura, his energy. This man had a dangerous streak she did not want to explore.

"I don't know," she answered honestly.

"I wouldn't hurt you."

The raspy sound of his voice lured her to trust him while suspicion kept her cautious. "Why? Because I'm a woman?"

"No. Because there's a certain frailty about you."

A frailty he could break if he wanted. Was her experience in Iraq so transparent?

"I'm asking you to tell me what you know about Habib," he said. "I'm asking."

He wasn't going to force her. That did something to her, cracked her defenses. He was leaving the choice up to her. She had a feeling she didn't know enough to do any damage, anyway.

"We got a tip that Habib has been contacted by someone in Lebanon a few weeks ago," she began. "A senior operative for Hezbollah we later discovered had been shot and killed. We had no way of knowing if Habib would be in contact with anyone else, but we suspected he would. Travis and I were sent to Monrovia to watch him. He's a diamond merchant who uses his market as a front. We're afraid he'll help finance a merger of splinter cells between Hezbollah and al Qaeda."

"Al Qaeda with Iranian government backing. Now there's a scary concept."

"Hezbollah does have strong Iranian support. The government considers them a legitimate resistance movement." She sipped her wine and put the glass down on the table. "Now you know what I know." She waited expectantly for him to tell her what he knew.

"You don't belong here," he said instead.

So, he was going to take the same angle as everyone else. He saw her frailty and wasn't going to bother to look deeper. "Who is Ammar Farid Salloum?"

"Tell McQueen there's no need to send in a rescue squad. I'll take you to the airport in the morning."

Anger rose up in her. "I'm not going anywhere until you tell me what you know."

"My cause is nowhere near as noble as yours. Go home. Tell McQueen if Ammar is behind the merger, it will never happen."

"Oh? And why is that?"

"Because once I have what I need from him, I'm going to kill him."

"Killing Ammar will stop the merger?"

He didn't answer, but a deadly gleam darkened his eyes.

"What do you need from Ammar?"

"You should find a job that's not so dangerous."

"What I do is none of your business. What do you need from Ammar?" she repeated.

"Why do you do it?"

"Answer me."

"Why does someone as fragile as you come to dangerous countries and chase terrorists?"

"Is Ammar a terrorist?"

He just looked at her.

"Is he Hezbollah?" she asked.

"What do you think?"

So Ammar was a Hezbollah terrorist. Nothing surprising there.

"I'm not fragile," she told him.

He pushed his chair back and stood. Moving with deliberate slowness, he came to stand beside her chair. She strained her neck to look up at him.

"No?" He reached to brush some hair behind her shoulder.

Haley tensed. Her heart flew.

He slid his hand around her arm and above her elbow, and coaxed her to stand. She hesitated. Another tug, and she gave in and stood. Taking her hands in his, he pulled her closer.

What was he doing?

She could feel the heat of him. That same insecurity swarmed her, the way it always did when she was too close to men who threatened her. A sense of helplessness. Lack of control. But there was something else pushing through the heaviness of her anxiety. Desire.

Seeing the way he watched her, she eased away from him. He let her hands go and she went into the open room and faced him.

He moved toward her, stopping an inch or two from her. Looking down into her eyes, he tore through layers with that strong gaze.

She struggled to keep from shrinking away.

"There's no room for fear against men like Ammar," he said. "What kind of fool lets you do it?"

"My job is to gather intelligence."

"And it almost got you killed."

He thought she was weak. Afraid. It grated on her. She worked hard to rise above what the insurgents had done to her. She'd trained hard. Built up her defenses, her self-confidence. But mostly she worked hard to never feel helpless or vulnerable.

The fact that this man considered her exactly that made her want to fight back. She wanted to show him she wasn't weak.

Knowing she'd catch him unprepared, she gripped his arm as she turned her back to him. With a move she'd practiced over and over, she sent him flying over her shoulder. His body crashed to the tile floor. As big as he was, he weighed a ton, but all she'd needed was skill and momentum. She grinned down at his surprised face.

"You don't scare me that much," she quipped.

He moved up onto his elbows. "I should."

And he swiped his feet so fast she couldn't jump out of the way fast enough. She fell and he sprang his powerful body onto her. With her legs clamped by his, she couldn't kick free. Snatching her wrists, he dragged them over her head as his full weight pressed her down on the cool floor. In an instant she realized the folly of trying to prove she wasn't afraid of him. She was afraid. She overcame it most of the time, but not now. Not with this man. His legs held hers in an unrelenting vice. She was trapped. Pinned. Panic welled inside her. No man had ever treated her like this. Manhandled her. Not since Iraq.

Flashes of terrible memory suffocated her. Something wild broke inside her.

"Get off me," she growled, squirming beneath him, fighting her panic, trying not to let it show.

He only watched her face. Curious. Dominant. A deeper memory began to surface. Oh, God. Her heart slammed into terrified beats. "No." She writhed and bucked but he held her effortlessly in place. "No. Let me go!"

The memory morphed into the face of an Arab man. Over her. On top of her. The sound of tearing clothes shook her. She squeezed her eyes shut and screamed. She didn't want to remember.

"No, no, no, nnnooooo!"

"Hey."

"Let me go. Please-let-me-go." She heard herself begging and couldn't stop. The Arab's face lingered, making her sick to her stomach.

"I'm not hurting you."

"Let me go." Tears sprang into her eyes. She was going to be sick.

Rem rolled off her. Shaking, she stumbled to her feet and ran to the bathroom. Blood left her limbs, leaving her trembling with pinpricks running up her arms and legs. She fell in front of the toilet, heaving air into her lungs. The Arab's face was imprinted in her mind. Over her. Leering. Speaking in that language that was so awful to her now.

She didn't throw up. But emptiness yawned inside her. She fell onto her hip and pressed her cheek against the cool wall, flattening her shaking hand beside her head. She closed her eyes and sobbed. Would it never leave her? Would she never be free of its hold on her?

"I don't want to remember," she wailed. "I don't ever want to remember."

Chapter 3

Rem stood in the bathroom doorway staring down at Haley. "What the hell?"

He moved closer, kneeling on one knee. "I didn't mean to hurt you." He reached to touch her shoulder, but she whimpered and cringed away from him.

The reaction stung. He was accustomed to people, women in particular, shying away from him. He hated how that always bothered him. But seeing Haley crumpled on the floor tore through his usual ability to remain immune. He'd been careful with her. He knew he hadn't hurt her. Not physically. Pinning her to the floor had triggered something horrible in her.

He reached for her once more. Slowly. "I'm not going to hurt you."

She cringed again, but he brushed the loose strands of her dark hair back from her face anyway. She looked at him with wide, terrified eyes. It ripped something away, more of his immunity. Ignoring her struggles and pitiful pleas, he lifted her into his arms and carried her from the bathroom. She pushed with her hands at his chest, but her resistance wasn't in earnest. Those awful whimpers. God, he'd never felt so wretched before, which was unbelievable. His life was full of wretchedness. He had a head full of bad memories. He couldn't remember a time when he'd actually felt happy. Well, once, but even that had ended badly.

Going into the living room, he sat on the couch and held her until she quieted against him.

I don't want to remember.

He understood that kind of pain. Knowing she suffered something similar made her a kindred spirit. No one had ever touched that part of him. But for some reason, Haley had.

She moved her head, tilted it until she met his teary, aquablue eyes, a much deeper blue than his own. Wariness lingered there, as though she questioned his intent now that she'd grown aware of how he held her. He didn't move, only held her loosely, not wanting her to feel trapped, and definitely not wanting to see that awful fear again. She met his gaze and gradually the wariness faded and a kind of curiosity took its place.

Feeling spread through him, warmth he seldom experienced. He wanted to know what lived within her beautiful, mysterious depth. But she drew too much from the bowels of his dark core. What he fought so hard to bury, she dredged to the surface with silent understanding, the recognition of what they shared. A darkness they both couldn't shed. As impossible as it seemed, this fragile thing in his arms made him reveal his weakness. He didn't need a mirror to know that.

Closing her eyes, she put her head on his shoulder. He felt her breaths on his neck. A roar of protectiveness mushroomed in him. He'd defended women before, but he swore, the way he felt right now, he'd go to his grave for this one.

Standing with her in his arms, he carried her toward his bedroom. He didn't think she wanted to be alone tonight. He didn't want to leave her alone. She kept her head tucked in the curve of his neck and shoulder. He left the lights off and put her on the bed, following her and drawing the covers over them both. She lay with her back to him, so he rolled to his side and put his arm around her. She didn't resist, which convinced him he'd been right. She didn't want to be alone, and trusted him not to cross any boundaries. He allowed himself to savor the closeness. He'd had a few moments like this in his life, but only a few. He'd enjoy them for as long as he could, because one thing he knew: it would never last.

The next morning, Haley woke to the sound of breathing. She turned her head on the pillow and found herself looking at Rem. His eyes were closed, still asleep. Despite the rugged planes of his face, he was a handsome man. She wondered what had put the lines of strain between his eyebrows. Wondered even more why she felt so drawn to him. How she'd been so comforted when he'd held her last night. It didn't make sense. She barely knew him, and what she did know didn't ease her mind. Far from it. Why hadn't she been drawn like this to someone like Travis?

Travis.

A twist of worry gripped her. Was he okay? It killed her, not knowing. He might be fighting for his life and here she was, lying in bed with a man she didn't know, having the hint of feelings she hadn't felt since before Iraq. This dark and dangerous man had pinned her down and unearthed memories better left buried, and then chased the ugliness away just by holding her.

Recalling his tender touch and the look in his eyes, she realized what had drawn her to him. He'd felt her agony. Maybe he'd lived some of his own at one time in his past. He'd comforted her because he understood the need. Not liking the warmth that made her feel, Haley pushed the covers aside and eased off the bed.

Now was a good time to try and call Cullen. Still fully clothed, she walked quietly out of the room and crossed the living room. She climbed the stairs to her room and sat on the bed. Looking toward the door, she listened. Nothing. Hopefully Rem was still sleeping. She didn't care if he knew she called Cullen; she just didn't want him near when she learned what Odie had probably discovered about him by now.

She lifted the phone.

"Haley." Odie sounded relieved when she got the call through. "Can you talk?"

"Yes."

"Hang on. Let me get Cullen. He's going out of his mind with worry."

Haley waited until Cullen got on the line.

"Are you all right?" he demanded.

"Yes. Rem is going to take me to the airport today, so you don't have to send anyone."

"We'll see about that."

Of course, he'd send someone at the slightest indication she might be in danger. "Have you found Travis?"

"He's going to be okay. He's in a German hospital, but he's stable enough to move to the States. We're in the process of getting him here."

Haley closed her eyes and leaned her head back, breathing with relief. "Thank God."

"When he found out you weren't with him, it took three doctors to strap him down."

"Make sure you tell him I'm all right."

"A lot of good that'll do. They'll probably have to sedate him to get him back to the States."

"I'm just glad he's okay."

"All of us are. Where is Rem right now?"

"He was still sleeping last I checked."

"Can you get away from him?"

"He said he's going to take me to the airport. All he wanted was information about why Travis and I were here." She left out what he'd gleaned after her first call to Odie. "Why? What's wrong?"

"Play along with him for now," Cullen said.

Foreboding moved through her. "What's wrong?"

Cullen didn't answer right away. "I don't want to scare you."

"You *are* scaring me. What did you find out about Rem?"

"He's got a rough history, Haley. I had a hard time digging anything up on him. Not surprising, though, considering he's never held a legitimate job."

A lump of dread clogged her throat and her heart beat faster. "What do you mean?"

"He was born in France and moved to the U.S. with his dad. But the dad died when he was fourteen and that led to an early career in drug dealing. Got caught in his early twenties and barely missed a prison sentence. Hooked up with a guy named Dane Charter after that, a real badass of a mercenary who started his own company. Ran jobs all over Africa. A few in the Middle East. Not always for governments, which means he played both sides of the line. I found a news article that mentioned Dane's company and told of all the atrocities his men committed while protecting diamond mines during the Sierra Leone war. Made a huge profit and got away clean. From what I can tell, Rem worked for Dane up until a few months ago, so you do the math."

She swallowed the lump of dread still in her throat. Rem was a mercenary who didn't care if he worked for rebels or governments.

"Is he…is he still…" She couldn't finish the question.

"Once a merc, always a merc. Especially that kind. One thing I found interesting: Dane was killed three months ago and his company closed. His wayward business practices must have finally caught up to him. Good riddance if you ask me.

Not sure what Rem is up to now, but it can't be for the good of humanity. Who knows, maybe he's independent now. Maybe there'll be another rogue private military company popping up on the map."

"What's he doing here, then?"

"Good question. I don't want you hanging around long enough to find out. If he's serious about taking you to the airport, let him. If not, get away from him as soon as you can. He's extremely dangerous, Haley. No hero in that résumé. I've been going crazy thinking a guy like that kidnapped you. And I don't have to tell you why. I know you're capable, but it's your history that concerns me."

"But…he hasn't done anything." Except save her and Travis's lives. And then there was this connection that had sparked between them. She didn't want to believe anything bad about him, yet here it was, staring her right in the face.

"Yet."

Cullen's single word finally penetrated. "What do you mean, yet?"

"Do you think he's serious about taking you to the airport?"

"Yes."

"Good. Don't press him. Go with him. Get away from him. I don't know why he's after Ammar, but I do know a guy like that won't let anything get in his way. Whatever he intends to do, I don't want you around when he does it."

"He said he was going to kill Ammar."

"Then I just might let him. But that changes nothing, Haley. I don't trust his motives, and that's why I want you home. Understand?"

"Yes."

"I'll put your backup on hold for now. I've got three operatives in Paris. You don't get on a plane today, I'm sending them after you."

"Okay."

"We'll talk when you get here."

"Okay."

He disconnected and she put the phone back on its cradle and left her hand there, her thoughts a jumbled mess in her head. She put her other hand on her stomach, worried that she was alone with an unscrupulous mercenary who'd started his career selling drugs.

Before this she could have believed he chased terrorists for similar reasons as she and Travis. Now she couldn't deny his reasons were different and had likely started with blood on his hands.

Standing, she headed for the stairs, looking over the railing for Rem. She didn't see him, and the villa was quiet. Downstairs, she started when he emerged from his office, his face a hard, angry mask. His fists were curled at his side.

"Have a nice chat?" he asked.

Fear sent her pulse flying. Had he heard her entire conversation with Odie and Cullen? "I—"

"Get packed. I'll drive you to the airport. I don't care where you go from there." With that he disappeared back into the office.

Haley stared at the spot where he'd stood. He must know what Cullen had told her, and yet he was still going to take her to the airport. The emotion that had radiated off him confused her.

Why was he so mad? Because she'd learned the truth? She could well understand why he wouldn't want anyone to know such unsavory details about him, but why would a coldhearted mercenary care one way or the other?

Haley got into Rem's SUV, and he turned the vehicle around on the circular driveway. He approached the iron gate, but instead of opening it, the guard came out of the shack and walked to Rem's window.

Rem rolled the window down.

"There's a gentleman waiting to see you. I told him you weren't taking visitors, but he refused to go before he spoke to you."

"Who is it?"

"He would not give a name."

Haley watched Rem hesitate. "Open the gate." When the guard headed back for the shack, he looked at her. "Stay here." He lifted the hem of his jeans and pulled out a Glock.

Getting out of the SUV, he closed the door and put the pistol in the waistband of his jeans at the small of his back, then strode toward the gate as it opened.

A man stood on the other side. Haley recognized him. It was the man who'd gone to Habib's market. Ammar. A black sedan with tinted windows was parked behind him and two armed men stood on the other side.

Ammar saw her in the SUV and smiled wickedly. Haley subdued a shudder and climbed out of the vehicle, staying behind the open door. She wasn't armed but she wanted to hear this conversation.

"Your doctor friend did not lie, I see," he said. "It has spared him his life."

"If you hurt him I'll have to kill you sooner than I planned," Rem said.

Planned? Why was he waiting and what was he planning? That only made what Cullen told her all the more convincing. He had secrets. Dark ones. He knew this man on a personal level. This terrorist.

Ammar's eyes narrowed but Haley could see he didn't discount Rem's threat. She didn't doubt Rem was a formidable enemy.

Ammar glanced at the guard standing outside the gate,

armed with an AK-47 that was presently aimed at him. He probably wished he could just mow down her and Rem with a spray of bullets right now. Next, his gaze moved to Haley. He studied her in an unabashed way of a man accustomed to owning his women. Haley had to stop herself from doing something juvenile, like flipping him off.

At last he turned back to Rem. "I see you've made another friend."

"Disappointed you couldn't get to her first?"

Ammar smiled again, but it didn't touch his eyes. "She's very beautiful."

Haley watched the way Rem tensed, wondering if he knew he'd given his emotion away. He cared what happened to Haley, and Ammar knew it.

"Where is the man she was with?" Ammar asked.

He meant Travis. Haley waited for Rem to answer, but he didn't.

"Is he dead?" Ammar pressed. "Your doctor friend said he sent him to a European hospital. Did he make it?"

"Of course he did," Haley said defiantly. How could he gloat over something like that?

Rem sent her a warning look.

Ammar's gaze went to her. "Tell me, why was he in the market?"

"The same reason I was outside of it," Rem said before she could reply.

"I doubt it's the same."

"I wouldn't be so sure about that. Your popularity is growing. Haven't you noticed?"

Ammar's expression tightened and he turned that anger on to Haley. "Who sent you here?"

"Wouldn't you love to know," Rem taunted. Haley looked at him. She could speak for herself, did he know that?

"So you've teamed up with her, then?" Ammar asked, but

didn't wait for a response. "Or is there another reason you brought her here—" he gestured toward Rem's villa "—to your private compound?"

Rem didn't comment, but Haley was sure he knew as well as she did why Ammar had pointed this out. Rem had saved her from Ammar's men, and then he'd taken her home with him, a beautiful woman who might need protection.

"Yes." Ammar sounded complacent. "If you only wanted to question her, you could have done that at the doctor's clinic. Instead, you do what you always do. You intervene where you should not. It is your only weakness, my friend. One that will bring you death."

"I'm not your friend."

"You forget how well I know you."

Rem cocked his head as though inwardly scoffing.

"What does she know?" Ammar asked, taunting. "About you, that is."

Haley wished she could see Rem's face.

"I think you've worn out your welcome," he said.

Rem's guard stepped closer, weapon ready. The men hovering near the car stepped forward, stopping when Ammar held up his hand, his gaze never leaving Rem.

"Is it worth that much to you?" Ammar pressed. "Her life?"

Rem said nothing.

Ammar looked at Haley and then back at Rem. "It wasn't once."

Still, Rem didn't respond, but Haley sensed his angry energy. What did Ammar mean? What was their history? Did it involve another woman?

"I grow tired of these games," Ammar said. "Leave her alone, one moment, I will kill her. Leave with her and never show your face to me again, I will not harm her."

With that, he turned and walked back to the waiting car,

climbing into the back and closing the door. His men followed. Tinted windows hid them from view.

When Rem turned and came back to the SUV, Haley saw the fury etching his features.

"Close the gate," he ordered the guard, who immediately went to comply.

Instead of getting into the SUV, Rem passed it and headed toward the villa.

Slamming the passenger door shut, Haley followed. "What are you doing?" she called to his back, trotting to catch up.

He didn't acknowledge her. Anxiety unnerved her. She followed him back into the villa. He went to the dining room table and braced his hands on the back of a chair, looking as though he were about to pick it up and hurl it across the room.

Haley left the front door open and stopped next to him. "What was that all about?"

He turned his head, angled with the way he leaned on the chair, eyes shadowed and feral.

"How do you know him?" she asked.

Pushing off the chair so that it rocked off balance, he turned as he straightened. She should run now. The door was open. The keys were still in the SUV. But the gate was shut.

She stiffened when he moved toward her. Sensing he deliberately crowded her, she lifted her chin and met his eyes despite the instinct telling her to get away from him.

His anger smoothed and resignation took its place. "I should have killed him the first time I saw him."

"Why didn't you?"

He absorbed her face with those icy blue eyes and took his time replying. "We can't stay here anymore."

Alarm zapped her as he headed for his bedroom. *"We?"* She went to stand in the doorway of his room, where he gathered his belongings and shoved them into a duffel bag. "I thought you were taking me to the airport."

"Change of plans," he said matter-of-factly, and without looking at her. "You're coming with me now."

What? "No, I'm not. You said you were taking me to the airport. I want you to take me to the airport."

He straightened with the duffel in hand. "No can do. You're coming with me if I have to tie you and drag you."

Haley stared at him, chilled by the certainty in his tone. With heart hammering, she pivoted and marched to the door. Outside, she ran to the SUV. Passing it, she went into the guard shack.

"Open the gate."

The dark-skinned man with an untrimmed mustache stared at her. "Mr. D'Evereux said not to unless he tells me."

She looked at the controls and spotted what had to be the one to open the gate. Going forward, she reached to press the control before the guard could stop her.

The gate began to open.

When she ran back outside, the gate was already closing again. She saw Rem bend into the driver's side of the SUV. He came back up with the keys.

Haley went to him. "Give them to me and tell your guard to open the gate." She held out her palm.

He only turned his back and started back toward the villa. Behind her, she heard the gate finish sliding shut. This was making her really mad. Who the hell did he think he was?

Walking faster, she caught up to him and went for the keys. He held them tight in his grip. He clasped his other big hand around her wrist and easily pried her off him. Keeping hold of her, he continued his trek toward the villa. She tugged against him, but he forced her toward the open front door. There, he let go of her wrist and pushed her inside.

She stumbled as he kicked the door shut. Regaining her

balance, she darted around him. Yanking the door open, she ran for the guard shack. Screw the SUV. She'd run down the street until she found a car.

She heard Rem's chase, his heavy footfalls eating up the ground between them. She knew the moment he caught up to her that she was doomed. He hooked one arm around her. She stumbled and had to slow. He lifted her off the ground. Her back pressed against his chest. She kicked and wiggled and grunted. He lowered her enough so that she could put her feet on the ground. She tried to wrench herself out of his grip. Their feet got tangled and they both lost their balance.

"Damn it, woman!"

They rolled on the dirt and gravel, him blocking all her tactical moves and joining his grunts to hers, adding a few choice swear words. She wound up on her back with him on top. Before he could see it coming, she punched him. Blood sprouted from his nose.

"You can't make me stay here!"

Ignoring his bleeding nose, he tossed the SUV keys aside and pinned her with both arms and clamped her legs in the coil of his. She couldn't take a deep breath. She couldn't move much, either.

"Stop," he growled, as breathless as her.

She gave him a head bang, aiming her forehead for his already battered nose.

"Ah!"

"Let me go!"

He put his face just above hers and willed her with his eyes. "Stop fighting me."

"Then let me go!"

"Stop fighting me," he repeated.

She slowed her struggle.

"Please," he softly said.

Looking up into his intense, incredibly light blue eyes, she went still.

"I have to keep you safe," he added.

That finished her. She breathed hard a few times, until her pulse slowed and she relaxed. He believed Ammar would carry out his threat. And it dawned on her that he truly cared what happened to her—this man with such a dark past. It intrigued her. All his badness hadn't frozen his heart completely. Something warm curled through her.

Holding both of her hands in one of his, he used the back of his forearm to wipe the blood from under his nose. He wouldn't have had to hold her hands. She wasn't going to fight him anymore. She wouldn't get past the gate before he stopped her anyway.

He used both hands to pin her wrists again. Odd, how it didn't frighten her the way it had before.

"I've never met a woman like you," he said with exasperation, the rasp in his tone entirely too appealing. "I'm not sure if I should be impressed or worried."

"Definitely worried," she said, smiling.

He chuckled.

Seeing the change in his expression, she resisted the pull on her heart. She did not want to find him attractive. But he was. It seemed the longer she was with him, the more she liked him.

"You have to let me go," she said, amazed at how at ease she was underneath his heavy weight.

The smile left his eyes. "I can't."

"Cullen will send operatives after me."

"They won't find you."

"Where are you taking me?"

"Not to the airport."

"You can't force me to stay with you, Rem."

"I'm going to keep you alive. You heard Ammar. He'll kill

you. The moment I turn my back, he'll come for you and make sure I find out. I can't let him do that."

"What do you want that's so important? If you walk away, he'll leave us both alone."

"Is that what you would do? You'd walk away from a terrorist and let him carry on with his plan to kill as many infidels as he can?"

"Cullen won't let Ammar get away with anything."

"Cullen." He said the name derisively. "I don't need anyone else to fight my battles."

"Why is it so important for you to catch Ammar?" she asked again.

Something crossed his eyes that softened them, some kind of reminder of why he was here. She didn't think he would answer, but he did.

"He took something from me," he said.

"What did he take?"

His body sagged a little. He lowered his head beside hers, close to her neck. She heard him inhale. When he breathed out she felt the warm air on her neck. She turned enough to see his eyes were closed. When he lifted his head and opened them, she saw pain. Tragic pain. The same as she'd seen last night, a reflection of her own.

Releasing her, he rolled away and climbed to his feet. She sat up and watched him walk to the keys, bend and lift them. Stuffing them into his pocket, he walked over to her.

He extended his hand. "Please, Haley. I need you to come with me. Don't make me lose more than I already have."

Her heart melted all over his words, all over the way he looked down at her. She couldn't stop it, this feeling growing inside her. What it was, where it came from, she didn't understand. While everything Cullen told her about him kept her wary, she gave Rem her hand. He pulled her to her feet.

"All right, but you have to tell me where we're going," she said.

"To intercept a diamond deal."

Chapter 4

"I should call Cullen."

Rem glanced at her as he drove the SUV toward Robertsport. The sun was setting on another hot, dry day. The rainy season would begin soon. "Right. McQueen. The superhero soldier America loves so much."

She cocked her head as she looked at him, not missing his sarcasm. The man sure had a sore spot. She wondered what put it there. "He'll worry. And he told me he's sending three operatives after me if I don't get on a plane today."

"He sent you here to gather information. Well, you're about to get more than you bargained for. Go ahead and call him. Tell him to back off his team. Satellite phone's in my duffel."

She eyed his surly profile. "He's a good man."

"They all are."

"What's that supposed to mean?"

"Big-shot soldier. Ex-Delta. All that." He smirked.

"Boy, somebody has a chip on his shoulder." He didn't look at or acknowledge her. But she could feel the annoyance radiating off him. "Did you want to be a soldier?"

He turned at that. "I was too busy selling drugs, remember?"

She couldn't think of a thing to say. Of course, he'd heard her conversation, but it had gotten under his skin like a big ugly tick. "Were you?"

"I was fourteen."

"So blame the world, why don't you." She shook her head and crawled between the seats, not caring that her butt was prone. How had she ever been drawn to such a sourpuss? *Note to self: watch your low moments.*

She dug inside his duffel, spotted the satellite phone and hesitated. There were other things packed in the duffel. Ammunition. A knife in a holder. Packages of dried food. Extra clothes. Seeing a portion of what looked like the black handle of her P99, she pulled it up from the bottom of the bag and stared at it. At least she knew where it was now. Tucking it back under the contents of the bag, she retrieved the satellite phone and was about to withdraw when she noticed a partially unzipped compartment. Seeing something inside, she unzipped it the rest of the way and pulled out a photograph. A stunning woman with long, dark hair and dark eyes smiled for whomever took the photo. She stood in front of a brick ranch home in the fall of some year. Disconcerted by a sudden rush of jealous curiosity, Haley tucked the photo back into the pocket and zipped it shut.

Climbing back into the passenger seat, she caught Rem adjusting the rearview mirror. She narrowed her eyes at him. Had he lowered it to check out her butt or keep an eye on what she found in the duffel?

She entered the number and waited.

"Odie," she said, when the woman answered.

"Let me guess, you aren't boarding a plane today," Odie said.

"Let me explain."

"Cullen's going to blow a gasket."

"Cullen is wrong about Rem, Odie." She ignored Rem's slow glance her way, feeling his surprise.

"You say 'Rem' like you're getting cozy with him."

Haley sighed her impatience. "Go get Cullen."

"Didn't take you long to get on first-name basis. It's very... interesting, especially for you." Haley heard the curbed teasing in her tone. Dryly she wondered what it cost the otherwise crass woman to hold back. She had to be dying to jab about what she perceived as Haley's new love interest.

That didn't mean Haley didn't use these opportunities to her advantage. "Not nearly as interesting as your phone conversations to that guy on the East Coast."

Odie *humphed*.

Haley laughed. "Isn't he kind of soft for your usual taste?"

"Beats the he-men that are always coming and going from this place. Thank the Universe they're in the field most the time."

It wasn't the first time she'd heard Odie talk like that about men. "What do you have against operatives?"

"They think they can have any woman they want, yet they're all retarded when it comes to relationships."

"Somehow I can't picture you wanting a relationship. That guy you met must be something."

"He is. But what I like about him most is he's *normal*."

"Cullen said he's an engineer."

"What's wrong with that?"

"Nothing, I—"

"It's a refreshing change," Odie all but snapped, interrupting her in the process.

It would never last. Not only did Haley hear it in her friend's tone, but Odie with an engineer was just laughable.

"You'll be back at TES in no time," she said.

"Yeah, yeah. And you'll be leaving it. It's like Cullen all

over again. You're falling all over that guy instead of paying attention to your mission."

Before Haley could argue, Cullen got on the line. "Where are you?" He sounded furious.

"Calm down. I'm *fine*."

"Where are you?"

She had to tell him. "On our way to Robertsport."

"We?"

Haley stayed quiet. This wasn't going to go well.

"I'm sending in a team," Cullen said.

"No. Don't do that. Just trust me on this, okay? This is turning into something big."

"Exactly what I *don't* need to hear. Let me talk to him."

"What?" He wanted to talk to Rem? Should she let him?

"D'Evereux. Put him on."

After hesitating a couple of beats, Haley handed Rem the phone. He raised a brow and she shrugged.

He took the phone. "Yeah."

His eyes shifted to Haley and she could all but hear Cullen threaten him.

"The last thing I want is anything to happen to her," he said after a while. "It's the reason I'm taking her with me…I don't have a choice…believe me, I wanted to get her on that plane as much as you did."

A longer silence passed. If Haley knew Cullen, he was demanding information from Rem. She watched as Rem relented.

"Yes, his name is Ammar Farid Salloum," he said at last. "You wondered if Habib Maalouf was into terrorist financing, well, you were right. But it goes a lot deeper than that. Ammar's the one you want, not Habib. Ammar's been threatening Habib for years. Holding the lives of his family over his head if he doesn't do what he wants. Usually that's laundering money through the purchase of diamonds." He paused. "That I can't tell you."

What had Cullen asked? What couldn't he tell anyone?

"I'll get Ammar. That's all you need to know," Rem said.

Haley heard Cullen's raised voice from across the vehicle but couldn't decipher what he said.

Rem glanced over at her before facing forward again. "I understand your concern, but there's nothing I can do about it. If you believe nothing else I tell you, believe that Ammar will find Haley no matter where she goes. He'll find her and he'll kill her."

He paused again as Cullen spoke on the other end of the connection. "I know Ammar. Better than I want to know him. He won't try anything as long as Haley's with me."

Was Ammar afraid of Rem? Judging by the long silence, Cullen was wondering the same thing, or else he'd realized he wasn't going to win the argument. Rem wasn't budging. And if someone as disreputable as Ammar was afraid of him, he must be more dangerous than any of them imagined.

She was still grappling with that and the notion that he knew more than he was saying when he handed her the phone.

"He asked for you," he said. "Not too kindly, either."

She took the phone and Rem faced the road as though nothing unusual had occurred.

"Cullen?"

"I don't like how personal it is for him. He won't even tell me why he's after Ammar."

The picture of the woman flashed in her mind. "Don't send anyone, Cullen. Not yet. Let's see where this leads over the next couple of days."

"Out of the question."

"Cullen—"

"I'm not leaving you with a guy like that. I don't trust him."

"He isn't going to hurt me."

Silence.

"I can gather information." It was the closest she could come to letting him know she'd picked up on the fact that Rem might be withholding something big from them.

Cullen didn't say anything. She could tell he still wasn't convinced, but he was beginning to waver. Haley was his only inside source at the moment. He wanted to maintain that, but he didn'want her at risk.

"I'm safe with him, Cullen. You know that," she coaxed.

"You're anything but safe, Haley. I want you back here."

"Well, I don't want to come back yet. I want to see what else I can dig up on Ammar and anyone he's associated with."

"Precisely why I want you back here. I don't want you going any further with this."

"You wouldn't have sent Travis and I to Monrovia if you didn't think there was something worth pursuing."

"You're alone now. Travis isn't with you."

"I'm not a victim anymore. When are you and Travis going to get that?"

Cullen sighed hard, the size of his frustration reaching her from across the miles separating them. "I'm posting some men in Monrovia. They'll be at the Mamba Point Hotel."

"Cullen—"

"You have forty-eight hours before I tell them to go after you. And my order is going to be shoot to kill without asking questions. Understand?"

"Yes." It was the best she'd get from him.

She said goodbye and held the phone in her lap. Beside her, Rem stayed quiet and kept his attention on the road.

"Who is she?" she asked.

As she expected, that brought his head around. The abruptness of it.

"The woman in the picture," she explained. "It was in the zipper comp—"

"I said get the phone, not snoop around in my things," he said, cutting her off.

She decided not to mention that her gun didn't belong to him. "I know she's the reason you're doing this." She hesitated. "Now that you're dragging me into your mess, I have a right to know who she is."

"Was."

Did that mean she was dead? Haley had to push back her sympathy. "Who was she?"

His hand tightened on the wheel.

"You must have loved her," she pressed.

"She was my sister."

Haley began to see the resemblance, except for the woman's dark eyes. "What happened?"

He didn't respond and she didn't make him. She could feel his anguish. See it in his profile. "Ammar killed her, didn't he?"

Still, no response.

"Why?"

"Enough questions, Haley." He drove to a stop in front of a shack of a building.

She didn't force the issue. Little by little his puzzle was unraveling, and it contradicted his character. He seemed so trustworthy, yet his past was far from redeeming. And he clearly had something to hide. He didn't pretend to deny that fact, either. He didn't care who knew he wasn't revealing everything. He wasn't going to bend.

Well, she wasn't leaving his side until she uncovered whatever made him feel so threatened. She just hoped that when all was said and done he'd be standing on the right side. Her side. She didn't think her gut was wrong about him, but then, why was he guarding his secrets so well?

Getting out of the SUV, she looked closer at the run-down building. If one could call it a building. It didn't even look like it could keep out the rain. "What's this?"

"Our new accommodations." He turned a wry grin her way. "It's a step down from the last one."

She took in the chipping blue paint and cracking concrete, and moved on up to the rusting metal roof. "Welcome to Liberia." She stepped into the place behind him. "Why are we here? In Robertstown, I mean."

"Habib comes here to meet his diamond contact."

"So after he gets the diamonds we…what? Follow him?" She saw the two single beds and ramshackle chair and grimaced. "Is there running water?"

"If I hadn't met you, Haley, I'd have never believed a woman like you existed. No, there's no running water, but we'll only be here one night."

What did he mean by that? What kind of woman did he think she was? "In other words, yes." Did he think she was smart for figuring out what he intended? Or was there something else about her that struck him?

He sent her a questioning look.

"We're going to follow Habib?"

Rem broke his gaze from hers and went back to the SUV. He returned with a box and put it on a counter in the open kitchen area. She leaned over the box. Lantern. Freeze-dried food. A bottle of booze.

"Are you always this prepared?" She'd let him evade her questions for now.

He pulled the bottle of whiskey from the box. She lifted one brow. Just like a true-to-form gunslinger, he removed the cap and swigged. Then slouched onto the only chair in the dirty place.

The last of daylight had all but faded to darkness. Around here, only the stars and moon provided light. Removing the lantern from the box, she put it at the end of the counter and lit it, all the while feeling Rem watch her.

She took out the freeze-dried food and began to prepare a package of beef stroganoff. Yuck.

"At least we won't starve," she quipped.

"Haven't you ever eaten like that before?"

She nodded. "Yes. In the Army."

He was quiet for a while.

"Why'd you quit?" he finally asked.

A little zap of a shock bit her. She never talked about this. She stopped opening the package and glanced at him. Was he asking because she'd questioned him about his sister? Did he feel he could now? That he was allowed? No one had ever asked her about Iraq. Not directly and not since she had to when Army officials questioned her.

"What happened to you?" he asked. And when she still didn't reply, he added, "Is it the reason you do what you do?"

"Look, I don't bug you on your issues, so do me a favor and don't bug me on mine."

His mouth closed and he just met her gaze. Then he said, "Angie was killed because of me."

She abandoned the package of freeze-dried food and gave him her full attention. "Why?"

Again, he just met her gaze.

"What happened?"

"I interfered with the wrong people."

"Ammar?"

"He was one of them."

"So, your sister was killed because you tried to do something good? Something right?"

"You don't know me," he said, annoyance giving his tone an edge.

"Terrorists deserve to die." This time it was her who couldn't keep the emotion out of her voice.

"It doesn't matter what they are to me."

She searched his face for a lie and didn't find one. He wasn't discriminating about who he killed. If they crossed his path…

It sent a shiver of foreboding through her. She turned back to the package of freeze-dried food and dumped it into a bowl. Maybe she was wrong about him. Maybe this feeling she had—that he'd been thrown into circumstances that had gotten out of control—was off.

"What did you do in the Army? Before you went to work for the great and honorable Cullen McQueen?" he asked.

"What's wrong with being great and honorable?"

"Nothing, so long as we don't confuse controversial with honor. I've never understood why men like me get the bad reputation while men like McQueen get all the good press. We do the same thing, really. Kill people for shady causes. My missions may not have always been for the governing side, but I always knew who the innocents were."

"Then you aren't any different than other men who fight for humanity."

He grunted and sipped more whiskey.

"What happened with your sister?" she asked.

"What happened to make you work for a secret counterterror outfit?"

She wasn't hungry anymore. "You want to eat, make your own dinner." She went over to one of the single beds and debated whether she wanted to lie on it. When was the last time it was washed? Who'd lain on it last?

"Answer my question, I'll answer yours," he said.

A familiar, ugly sensation filled her. What scared her most was she felt compelled to tell him. That connection thing again. That feeling they had something important in common, no matter how grim its source. Would telling him help her let go? Why him? Why couldn't it have been Travis?

Travis had never pushed her. He was always too careful with her. Rem was…different. He didn't coddle her. Didn't treat her like a victim.

"I don't remember all of it," she finally said, unable to stop whatever drew her. "I was a field artillery surveyor in the Army when our convoy was attacked." What came next was a lot harder to say. She turned and sat on the bed, looking down at the floor. The last time she'd told anyone this was after her rescue. She'd never repeated it to anyone. "Our vehicle was trapped by debris after an explosion. We were overtaken by insurgents while we were stopped. Everyone was killed but me." She hesitated. "Two of the insurgents captured me."

Rem leaned his head back on the chair and didn't interrupt her.

Images of the two insurgents coming after her were forever emblazoned in her mind. "They took me to an abandoned building and used their guns to beat me. I don't remember what happened after that." But that was where patches of the terror haunted her. "The next thing I do remember is a group of soldiers coming into the building and carrying me out on a stretcher. I was flown to a German hospital where I was treated, then sent home." She couldn't speak about what the doctors had told her. About the horrific abuses her body had suffered and that her mind had blocked out.

Rem didn't ask if she was raped and that relieved her. She didn't think she'd be able to answer, anyway. It was still too painful to face.

She was glad for the dim lighting in the small but open dwelling. Rem hadn't moved. He still leaned his head back on the chair, bottle of whiskey in his hand and resting on one thigh.

"I was on assignment in Argentina about three months ago,"

he said. The sound of his voice was low and gruff but a little vulnerable. Odd for a man his size and with his demeanor. "We were supposed to be guarding a cattle ranch that was having trouble with rebels. At least, that's what I was told. I never did see any sign of rebel activity while I was there."

He paused and she wondered if he'd continue. "It sounds dangerous," she said.

"Dane made it worth my while."

"You made a lot of money?"

He sipped some whiskey and put the bottle back on his thigh. Of course, she knew he had. His villa proved it.

"Who is Dane?"

"One night I was on patrol when I caught one of the ranch workers raping a woman," he said without answering. "When the guy fought me, I shot and killed him. Dane Charter, the one behind Charter Security, reprimanded me for it. He said whatever the ranch workers did was none of our business. That's when I started to get suspicious about him. It wasn't the first time I'd noticed something odd on assignments. When I got back to the States, I stopped working for him."

"You stopped working for him because you were suspicious?" It didn't seem like enough of a reason.

"He was into drug dealing. Cocaine."

She searched his face. Why did she get the feeling he wasn't telling her something? "Is that what the ranchers were doing?"

"Yes."

"How do you know?"

"I saw the drugs."

"Where? When?"

"On that last assignment."

Was he being deliberately vague? "What did you do?"

"What was I supposed to do?"

Not walk away. She hadn't known him long, but Rem walking away from anything didn't wash.

"How does your sister fit into all this?" she asked.

"The man raping the woman in Argentina was someone Ammar knew, a business partner. In retaliation, he had a couple of his friends pay a visit to my sister." He hesitated. "They killed her."

Haley closed her eyes to the horror she could so imagine. He didn't have to tell her details. She knew them. When she opened her eyes, she saw Rem had put the bottle of booze aside. He stood with that fluid movement of his and came over to the bed. Sitting down on the other side of it, he lay on his back. When he opened his arm in silent invitation, she hesitated. If he was withholding information from her, should she trust him? If she wasn't so tired, maybe not. But she was, and thinking about Iraq had her dreading the night. Putting her questions aside for now, she lay against him.

The warmth that enveloped her came from more than his body heat. How could it feel so right being so close to him? She didn't want to analyze it. Tonight she'd let herself fall into this contentment. Tomorrow, she'd listen to her mind.

Haley sat with her feet on the chair, holding a cup of coffee in front of her bent knees, unable to stop looking at Rem. He leaned against the wall next to a window, staring across the street, surveying the road and the tangle of jungle beyond. She was supposed to be distancing herself today. But the feelings from last night still circled her heart. They'd shared something intensely personal. And now they were closer.

His defensiveness against men of Cullen McQueen's caliber made a convincing argument that was what he craved most in life. To be honored. To be honorable. But the truth couldn't be changed. He was a drug dealer turned mercenary. Where was the honor in that background?

He was the epitome of the kind of man who usually frightened her. Who ought to frighten her now. And yet… something drew her to him. Was it the tragic loss of his sister? Had the experience changed him and that was what she saw? He'd come here to hunt down a terrorist—a worthy endeavor, to be sure—but what would happen once he found his retribution? Would he ever find it? Or would he return to his mercenary ways?

"How do you know Habib will be here?" she asked.

He glanced back at her and then resumed his surveillance. "I've followed him before."

"But how do you know he'll be here today?"

"I heard him arrange it."

"How? When?"

"After Ammar threatened Habib at the market. After you and Travis were attacked."

While she lay unconscious? She stared at the back of his head. "Who is Habib meeting? Who is his diamond contact?"

"Somebody from a small-scale mining company outside Koidu. Easier to smuggle from a smaller outfit than the bigger ones. Less money for security. And Habib probably has tighter connections with them."

"So, what were you planning? If you want revenge, why not just kill Ammar? Why snoop around his illicit diamond deals?"

Rem didn't answer and a few seconds later, he straightened from the wall. "He's here."

She swore in French, something she only did when she was really frustrated. She wanted him to answer her.

Rem glanced back at her, a frown of momentary curiosity changing the set of his eyes before returning his attention to the window. Well, it was good to know he spoke French, too. She only knew it because her mother was French.

Haley put the cup down and unfolded her legs from the chair to stand. At the window beside Rem, she watched Habib climb out of a white Jeep splattered with red dirt. His short black hair messed in the hot breeze, showing a round bald spot on the top rear of his head. The wiry, under-six-foot man glanced around him before disappearing into the building across the street. She looked up at Rem.

"What are we really doing here?" she asked. He hadn't answered her when she asked why he was snooping around Ammar's illicit diamond deals. Why?

Barely making eye contact with her, he left the window and began to load the SUV, which he'd parked beside the shack of a dwelling, hidden behind some trees.

Haley's instinct warned her something wasn't right. Rem was up to something, and it wasn't just getting Ammar.

After putting on her hiking boots, she got into the SUV and tried to calm her rushing adrenaline. Maybe she could go back to the Mamba Point Hotel. Walking back to Monrovia alone and unarmed would be nothing short of stupid. So for now, she was stuck with him.

He drove to a dirt road just outside Robertsport and turned around so the SUV faced the main road to Monrovia. Less than thirty minutes later, Habib's Jeep passed. The road was lightly traveled.

Rem waited awhile before driving onto the road.

"What are you going to do?" She knew it was futile asking.

His eyes never flinched from the road, and he pressed the gas when the Jeep came into view. Veering into the opposite lane, he raced beside the Jeep. Haley saw Habib's shocked and frightened look before Rem steered the big SUV right into the Jeep's side. Habib lost control with the hard hit and swerved off the road. A loud bang penetrated the interior of the SUV when the Jeep hit a tree. Rem braked and spun the

SUV around, racing back toward the Jeep. Her seat belt jerked her around in the seat. He skidded to a stop not two feet from the driver's door. Habib was slouched in the driver's seat.

Rem yanked off his seat belt and leaned close to her. "Stay here. If you run, I'm coming after you."

She heard her own rapid breaths as she stared at him with disbelief swimming so hard in her it made her dizzy. He was crazy. She should have never trusted him. He swung the driver's door open and ran to the Jeep. After searching Habib's clothes, he pulled the man's body back against the seat and leaned across him, then backed out with a small purse-sized leather pouch in hand.

While he loosened the top to check its contents, Haley swung the passenger door open. She went around the front of the SUV. "Did you kill him?" Her heart hammered wild and hard in her chest.

"Get back in the SUV." He grabbed her arm and forced her away from the Jeep.

"We can't just leave him here!"

"He'll be all right."

"Is he alive? Did you check?"

"He's alive. That crash didn't kill him, it only knocked him out."

"Did you check? Don't you care?"

Dark fury raged in his impossibly blue eyes. "How could I? Is that what you're thinking?" He shoved her back against the back passenger door of the SUV. "I saw him breathing. Get in, or I'll throw you in the back."

She slithered onto the passenger seat, feeling a tremble racking her legs and arms. Rem put the leather pouch in his duffel bag and climbed into the driver's seat. There were a lot of diamonds in there. Turning the SUV around, he accelerated. Ninety miles an hour down a two-lane, poorly maintained road, maneuvering curves, passing one car. He watched his rearview mirror. A few minutes later, he slowed. At a dirt road, he turned. She was jostled for more than an hour over the badly pocked road, until he finally slowed and searched the trees. Then he veered right into the dense vegetation, parking when it would let him go no farther.

She gaped at him, wondering what he was doing.

"Don't take anything with you," he said. "I packed enough for both of us."

Oh, God. Where was he taking her now? The operatives Cullen was sending wouldn't find her.

She jumped out of the SUV and onto soggy ground. All around her thick canopy shaded the sunny sky. Birds sang and called.

Rem grabbed the duffel bag where he'd stowed the diamonds as well as a second duffel bag, which he threw at her. She caught it, and he took her hand. Pulling her after him, he ran through the vegetation the SUV had flattened on the way in. They reached the dirt road. Putting the bag down, he unzipped it and pulled out a remote control. A detonator, she realized, and she could only gape at him when she heard the explosion through the thick vegetation. He'd blown up the SUV. Now they were on foot in the middle of a Liberian jungle.

Zipping the bag, he stood with it in his hand and pulled her after him again, running down the road.

No wonder he was so moody after Ammar had threatened him. He'd known all along that he'd have to take her with him. He wanted her on a plane and out of his life because he was playing a dangerous game with terrorists. There were too many diamonds in that leather bag for Ammar to let go. There had to be thousands and thousands of carats' worth.

What was he going to do with them? She had to stay with him to find out. Not that she had any choice.

Fifteen minutes later, she stumbled and tripped after him as he once again led her into the tangle of trees and vegetation that bordered the road. Then he let her go as he began pulling leafy branches off what she soon saw was a Jeep. A battered, rusting, once-dark-green Jeep. She climbed into the passenger seat. There was no seat belt, so she grabbed hold of the roll bar as he maneuvered the vehicle out of the jungle and back onto the road. He drove like a wild man, veering to the right when the road Y'd, veering again, this time left, when it Y'd again.

She dared a glance at him. His face was a hard mask of determination and grit. A pothole sent her entire body off the seat. She looked forward. And was shocked to see a village come into view.

Rem drove all the way through and stopped the Jeep at a clearing. Just ahead sat an armed black helicopter with no markings.

"Where are we going?" she demanded.

Grabbing the duffel with the diamonds, he slid his long legs out of the Jeep without acknowledging her. Bringing the second duffel bag with her, she followed him.

"How many diamonds are in that bag?"

"Don't talk about that now," he retorted in a low, angry tone.

She spotted a young man who smiled hugely, showing white teeth against dark skin as he approached.

"Remy," the man greeted. "I glad to see you." He leaned in for a masculine hug and a couple of hard pats on Rem's back.

"Thanks for coming through for me," Rem said, when the man withdrew. He pulled out a wad of cash from his wallet. He counted several hundred. The man laughed and nodded his excitement. "It is easy to help you, Remy. You save my family this year. Most of my people, too." He indicated toward Haley with his head. "You no mention bringing a lady."

"Sorry. We don't have time. I'll be in touch as soon as possible."

The man nodded again but looked curiously at Haley. Rem took hold of her hand and pulled her toward the helicopter.

Climbing in, she dumped the duffel in the pod and lowered herself onto the copilot's seat. Rem started the bird. It was stripped of everything but the essential instruments and controls for the guns. The rotor roared loud after a few minutes. And pretty soon they lifted into the air.

Haley watched the jungle canopy pass below, numb to this incredible turn of events. She should have seen it coming. Should have known the diamonds were all that interested him. Was that how he'd have his revenge? By taking Ammar's diamonds? It was a huge blow. It would set the terrorist back substantially. If Rem got away with it. And judging by the direction they were flying, he wasn't going to. They were headed north toward Sierra Leone.

Rem began speaking into a radio. An accented voice answered, "Come ahead."

The canopy opened and a rudimentary landing pad came into view. Several buildings were scattered across roughly a ten-acre compound, with signs of ongoing construction. One of the buildings was of a fairly good size for this part of the world.

Seeing the massive wall that enclosed the compound and its gnarled barbed-wire topping, she tracked it to the gate, where armed guards stood outside a small building. More guards waited at the earthen landing pad. Unease churned into something living inside Haley. There were too many. She felt trapped. She'd felt the same when she'd seen the insurgents coming toward her.

"Rem." She no longer tried to hide her growing fear. She met his gaze across the space of the helicopter, hoping she wasn't so wrong about him that she'd let him drag her into something terribly dangerous.

He turned his head and met her gaze. "Just stay with me. You'll be fine."

Something in her expression must have clued him to the chaos building in her.

"I won't let anyone hurt you. You have to trust me on that."

"Who are these people?"

"I'll die before I'll let anyone hurt you. Do you understand?"

She hated how she had to pant for air. What if he did die?

"Haley."

Armed dark-skinned men surrounded the helicopter. She felt herself falling back into Iraq. In the armored vehicle. Gunfire. The insurgents coming toward her. She rolled her head back and forth against the back of the seat, trying to control her snowballing panic.

"Haley." Rem moved closer to her, kneeling by her seat and sliding his hands beside her face, his fingers curving to the back of her head and neck. Gently, he held her face still. But kissed her hard.

Then his eyes blazed energy that fired through her haze.

"Be strong," he said in a deep, gruff voice.

"Rem." Oh, God, she was wrong to think she could do this. To think she could be an operative like Travis. He'd been right all along. So had Cullen. She wasn't cut out for this. Not after Iraq. Her mind reeled out of control. She couldn't stop it. She panted more.

"Listen to me," Rem hissed, his hands giving her a firm but gentle shake. "You're my girlfriend. You speak French and no English. Don't say anything unless they ask you a question or address you in French. Leave all the English talking to me. Okay?"

She could only stare at him.

"How fluent are you?" he asked in French.

"F-fluent," she managed to say.

"Don't be afraid," he told her still in French, and then, "I'll protect you."

She wasn't sure she could trust him like that.

"You'll be fine if you speak only French. Okay?"

She nodded even though she was still so unsettled. "Okay. French."

He withdrew his hands from her head. "Just stay by me and do what I tell you. They all know me here. They also know if anybody touches you, I'll kill them."

She stopped breathing altogether. Because now she believed him. She also believed he'd done it before.

"How many diamonds do you have?"

"Close to ten thousand carats. All rough."

She felt her head go cold and closed her eyes. "Oh." It came out on a breath full of dread. They were in so much trouble.

"This is no time to fall apart," he hissed, harsher than before.

She opened her eyes and found his. "You should have told me what you were planning!"

"Yeah? If I had, would you have come with me?"

"No way!" she all but screeched.

"Yeah. And Ammar would have killed you because I *have to do this!*"

"What do you have to do? What is so important to you that you'd go this far?"

"There's no time to explain it now."

She glanced out the window of the chopper and saw the armed men waiting for them. A fresh wave of fear renewed her trembles.

She turned back to him. "You're crazy."

He met her eyes with hard laser sharpness that, absurdly, worked to ground her. "You're going to be okay."

"Can you promise that?"

He didn't answer. She knew he wouldn't be able to. She was going to beat the crap out of him as soon as they were alone. And, oh, was he ever going to do some talking!

"Come on." He stood. "Let's go."

He helped her to her feet and faced the door. She put her hand on his back for support, hoping her shakiness wouldn't be visible once they were out of the chopper. The support left her when he bent to lift the duffel bags. He gave her the same one she'd been charged with before and hefted the other over his shoulder. She tried not to think about all those diamonds in there. Jumping down from the helicopter pod, he reached his arms to help her. Over his head and shoulders, she could see at least twelve armed and unsmiling guards waiting.

Rem set her feet on the ground and turned with her, sliding his arm around her and pulling her close.

One of the guards came into stride with Rem as they cleared the still-spinning blades. "I'll take you to Locke."

Haley looked over her shoulder as she walked with Rem, seeing the guards follow and flank them. They walked a few minutes, away from the earthen helipad and toward the largest building she'd seen from the air. She spotted two cameras on the roofline. A man stood on a concrete patio, behind a decorative concrete railing. He was tall and lean and wore all white. White slacks, white short-sleeved silky shirt. His sunglasses and belt were black, though. So were his shoes. As she climbed the stairs with Rem, she noticed the deep creases beside his grim mouth and pocked skin everywhere else.

"You didn't mention bringing company," the man said.

Rem smiled crookedly, one man to another. "I wasn't planning to, but…" He looked down at Haley from across his shoulder.

Haley kept her expression void of her true reaction, which had her envisioning her fist smacking his stubbly jaw. Instead, she looked up at Rem and acted as though she hadn't understood him but had read his sexy smile and leaned closer.

Once they were alone, he would be a dead man if he didn't tell her everything.

"How did you come to meet a man such as this?" Locke asked Haley.

She pretended to glance uncertainly from him to Rem.

"She doesn't speak much English," Rem said. "Only French. Her name is Haley."

Locke turned to her and said in French, "I am Locke Merchant. Welcome, mademoiselle. I trust your trip here was… uneventful?"

Haley gave him her best rendition of a bimbo smile. *"Oui, merci."* Silently, she thanked her French mother for raising her to speak the language as well as her father's American English. "Rem promised an adventure in an exotic place. I can see he was not exaggerating. You have a lovely home. And in the midst of such deprivation. It is a true oasis. I must admit, I was skeptical until now."

"Then, please, make yourself at home." He bowed slightly.

She angled her head politely.

To Rem, he turned a warning look and said in English, "If any of my men see her wandering around alone, I'll have her shot."

"She'll be with me the entire time."

Locke gave her a once-over. Then he said to Rem in English, "She's a little boyish for your taste."

"You know how the roads can get away from Monrovia." Rem turned to Haley and said in French, "I'm sure she would like to freshen up. Wouldn't you, love?"

Haley made a show of delight lighting her face. "Oh, *oui,*

oui." She looked down at herself. "I am filthy!" She gave a little shudder with her shoulders and smiled for Locke.

He didn't smile back. Just motioned for two of the guards to come forward. "Show them to their room." Then to Rem, "We'll talk over lunch."

Haley didn't miss the animosity pouring off Locke. Whatever reason Rem had arranged to come here, it wasn't friendly. Hoping no one would search their duffel bags, she walked with Rem past the pool and into a lower-level rec room. Sprawling light tan and textured tile made up a rec room with a long corner bar and a sitting area. Through that and down a wide hall to the right, the guards stopped at a doorway, and one of them opened it.

"You have one hour," he said, as Rem passed and she followed him.

Rem closed the door when the guards walked away and checked the room for cameras and bugs. There were none.

Haley tossed the duffel bag she still held onto the bed and folded her arms, letting all her anger go into her eyes. "All right." She pulled one arm from the fold to point her finger at him. "You better start talking."

Chapter 5

Rem walked past her and put the duffel he carried onto the only bed in the room. Anger swirled hotter inside her.

"You aren't going to ignore me."

He calmly turned to face her.

"What is this place?" she demanded. "Who is Locke?"

"Locke Merchant of Merchant Diamond Company," he answered.

She stared at him as pieces fell together. "Wait. Don't tell me…the diamonds came from him." And Locke didn't know he had them. Yet.

Nothing changed in his eyes. They were as hard and unreadable as ever.

"How do you know him?"

"I was on assignment during the Sierra Leone war. Guarding the mine he now owns."

Her jaw dropped open on a tide of shock. *Now owns?* "Was he a *rebel* who took over a mine during that hideous war? You were paid to help the *barbarians* who slaughtered *innocent natives?*"

"Locke used the war to his advantage. He saw an

opportunity and took it. He wasn't fighting for either side. Only his own."

"And that makes it okay in your mind?"

"None of what happened here was okay."

"But…you just…stood aside and watched the atrocities?"

"I did what I could."

"Which was what? Protect a rebel as he stole a diamond mine from its legitimate owner?"

"He'd already taken over the mine when we arrived."

Could a man really be so cold in the heart? Rough childhood or not, was there no warmth left in him? Maybe there was, but he couldn't find it inside himself anymore. Years of hard living had made him lose touch. He seemed so indifferent. And then…not. He'd said he'd done what he could. What did that mean?

"Why are you here?" she asked. "Why is Locke Merchant important?"

"You'll find out soon enough." He turned to the duffel bag she'd carried here and rummaged inside. Pulling out a wisp of bright blue material, he faced her and sent it sailing toward her.

Catching it, she held it up and realized it was a slinky little sundress. Thin straps attached to a low-dipping bodice and the hem might—just might—reach her knees. A sinking weight hung in her stomach.

She flashed her gaze to him. "I can't wear this."

"I have one other, but it's the same result."

He didn't understand. "I can't wear this or anything like it." She walked to the bed and dropped the insulting scrap of cloth there.

"You have to. You can't wear what you have on."

She just stared at him while conflicting emotion roiled inside her. She didn't dress like that anymore. She couldn't.

"We aren't going to be here long. Wear the damn dress. Tomorrow morning we'll be on our way."

He picked up the dress and handed it to her, then lifted the duffel she'd carried here and handed her that, too.

"Everything you need is in there," he said. "Go get ready."

"Don't tell me what to do. I can't wear that disgusting thing."

"It isn't disgusting. It's a nice dress."

"When did you buy it?"

"I didn't. A girl I was seeing left it behind. Why do you have such an issue with wearing a dress?"

"You make a habit of collecting your lovers' clothes?"

He angled his head and his eyes told her he didn't appreciate her sarcasm. "No."

"What happened to her? Did you scare her so much that she ran off without packing?"

Now his mouth curved into a scowl.

She didn't care. "How many girlfriends have left their clothes behind to get away from you?"

"One. And she didn't run off. She just forgot a few things."

"In her haste to get away from you."

The scowl smoothed as he began to assess her in a different way. "Is that what you'd like to do? Run away from me?"

"I'm not wearing this." She fisted the dress in front of her for emphasis.

He studied her a few seconds, taking his time. She wondered what cleverness was working in his mind. Did he think she feared him? Did she?

No.

"What's wrong with the dress?" he asked at last. "Why are you so against wearing it?"

How could she explain? She didn't even want to. It was too

personal. It was too close to that deep pain left over from Iraq, a pain she fought so hard to conquer. Maybe too hard.

Unable to move to go get ready, she stood still and met his too-clever eyes.

"It's just for today," he said.

He didn't know how dressing sexy affected her, and she didn't want to tell him now. So she mustered her courage and went into the bathroom. It was silly. Why did something so harmless bother her so much? But ever since her recovery it had. She couldn't even wear a bikini. Not that she'd want to anyway, with her scars.

Twenty minutes later, she slipped into the blue confection and looked at herself in the bathroom mirror. Then quickly redirected her focus. She didn't want to see sexy in the mirror. It made her feel funny. Leaving her hair down, she put on some makeup. Not much, just enough to accent her eyes and lips. Her mouth was dry and her heart beat so fast it turned her stomach over itself. Her palms were sweaty and her face felt cold. How would she manage to pretend to be Rem's bimbo of a girlfriend with so much chaos wringing her insides?

Taking a deep breath, she opened the bathroom door and stepped into the room. Rem looked up from adjusting a gun holster over his bare skin and went still. She watched his eyes take in her body. It magnified her discomfort. She felt exposed. Vulnerable. There was nothing she hated more since her ordeal in Iraq than this feeling.

She slipped into some sandals and marched to the door. "Are you ready?"

He finished buttoning a short-sleeve shirt that covered his weapon. It irritated her because there was no room to hide a weapon in that terrible dress.

When he put his hand on her lower back, she flinched, jumping a step away from him and sending him a narrow look.

He cocked his head. "We aren't going to be very convincing with you cringing away from me like that."

"Then don't touch me."

"You're my girlfriend."

"Sounds like you have a problem that doesn't happen to be mine."

"Haley…"

She opened the door. No one was in the hall. Rem tried again to put his hand on her lower back. She flinched again, but this time faced him fully, not jumping away. No, she wanted to attack him. Defend herself.

She pointed her finger in front of his face. "Stop that!"

His mouth tightened as he studied her. Then he took hold of her arm just above her elbow and hauled her back into the room, slamming the door shut with his hand over and behind her head. He moved forward to force her back against the door. She felt crowded and on the verge of losing any shred of courage she had left.

He put one hand above her head and leaned close. "What's wrong?"

"I don't want you to touch me."

"It's more than that. What's bothering you?"

She closed her mouth. Of course, he'd recognized her reaction. She berated herself for not trying harder to hide it from him. But how could she? Despair sailed like high winds inside her. How could she bring herself to say it? That would lead to more, more memories she didn't want to surface. He'd already dredged up too many as it was.

"I've touched you before. What's this all about?" he insisted.

She closed her eyes briefly.

"Tell me."

She shook her head. "I'm fine."

"I'm going to have to touch you."

"You don't *have* to. It's just convenient for you that we're role-playing."

"No. It's not that. I don't want to get shot today. So I want to be convincing in front of Locke. Tell me what's eating at you." He looked down at the display of cleavage the dress exposed, firing her ire along with more pooling dread. "Is it the dress?"

"I never wear clothes like this."

"Why not?"

"After…"

He waited. "After what?"

"Iraq," she said in a pathetically tiny voice, and watched understanding soften his life-hardened eyes.

He lowered his hand and put both on her hips. She stiffened and curled her fingers around his wrists.

"I'm not doing anything," he said. But his hands moved around to her back and slipped low until he cupped her rear.

She started to lift her leg to knee him, but he must have predicted her reaction and blocked the attempt with his leg. She fisted her hands and tried to hit him, but he blocked that attempt, too. At least it got his hands off her ass.

He brought his face closer, his mouth hovering near hers. Incredible blue eyes soft with understanding, and more. It stilled her. He kissed her, a breath of a touch on her lips, moving with her in wordless communication. She flattened her hands on his chest and pushed. But not with much purpose. How could she with all the sensation falling around her like confetti? He settled her nerves with this kiss. Weird. That he should be the one who could do that to her.

Sliding his hand up her back, he held her closer and slanted his mouth over hers. She opened hers to accept the exploration. Fire exploded in her. He kissed her harder, and Haley didn't understand why or how this had sprung up between them. And she didn't want to think about it right now.

She laced her fingers through his black hair. Her breasts pressed against his chest. He moved his hand down her body, over the curve of her rear and back up again. She broke away from his mouth with a breathless gasp. What the hell? She watched him swallow just before giving her neck a wet kiss, tasting her with his tongue. Nothing had ever felt so good. Pure. Genuine. She wanted to soak it into her, let it wash away Iraq.

He sank his fingers into her hair, fisting the softness and pulling her head back before kissing her again. She moved her hands to his chest, her fingers flexing. Her breathing quickened. Warm shivers continued to assault her.

He told her in French how beautiful she was.

That made her open her eyes. The sweet eroticism heated her blood. She told him not to stop kissing her in the same language.

He obliged her. Softly at first, so that only their lips touched. But that wasn't nearly enough. She urged him on for more. He eased his way inside her mouth. A seductive ploy. The intimate touch of their tongues ignited something foreign to her, something she hadn't felt in so very long.

Gradually, she withdrew. He seemed to sense the encroaching limits of her long-buried passion and let her, opening his eyes and meeting hers, answering warmth chasing the demons of his past from his eyes. The true essence of him emerged, just a glimpse, but it was there. Like a small gift.

Slowly coherency returned. Realizing how deftly he'd settled her and that it had been deliberate, she stiffened. She couldn't let him think he had that kind of power over her.

She bumped her hips against his, trying to push him off her. She pushed with her hands on his chest, too, but the feel of hard muscle under his shirt overwhelmed her senses. Whatever had erupted between them wasn't finished. And he wasn't being deliberate anymore. This part was real. He was reacting to the way he felt, and it was not unlike how she felt for him.

When he pressed his body against hers, flattening her against the door, she didn't resist. She heard and felt his deep breath. Moving his mouth over hers, he touched her with his tongue. Tentacles of pleasure scattered everywhere in her body. She opened her mouth and let him have all of her.

Another breath rushed out of him and he groaned. It fueled her passion. She met his fevered kisses, wrapping her arms around him.

He slid his arms around her, too, his hands cupping her rear through the thin material of the dress. Lifting her, he pressed his erection against her, pinning her with his weight against the door. She hooked her legs around his hips, drawing back from his hot mouth to take a few panting breaths, amazed and thrilled that he could make her feel this way.

He swore in French.

She held his head between her hands, loving his smooth, black hair between her fingers, and planted soft kisses all over his face. She made love to his mouth with hers, not with her tongue, just her lips. Soft touches that sprinkled an indescribable sensation all the way to her core. It was so powerful it shook her back to reality.

Slowly she pulled back her face and opened her eyes. He met her look with an answering confusion and passion. Their breathing resounded in the room.

Wordlessly, he eased her feet down to the floor and stepped back. She slid her hands from around his neck, down his chest, and off him, mortification expanding inside her.

She'd never kissed any man like that before, not even before Iraq. How had Rem worked his way into her heart like this? How had he breached the walls that Iraq had erected? She didn't understand. She felt confused and disoriented.

His smoldering eyes watched as though reading her while

his passion slowly ebbed. She welcomed the time to adjust her own equilibrium. She watched a familiar hardness come over him.

She used that to her advantage, too. It made her mad. How could he turn off his emotion so easily? Did all men have that ability, or was Rem better than most? She didn't care.

She pointed her finger in front of his face, feeling like it was becoming a regular gesture. "Don't do that again."

"If you want to make it out of here alive, don't flinch when I touch you," he shot back.

He'd kind of cured her of that, hadn't he? And did he think she hadn't noticed his investment in that kiss right along with her? "Don't touch my ass again. I'll drop you if you do. I don't care who sees it."

"Duly noted." He opened the door and followed her into the hall.

A guard approached. Their hour must be up. Haley willed away the insecurity still swimming in her stomach and let Rem put his hand on her lower back as she walked with him toward the guard.

They were led to the patio, where a table was set. Music played, a tropical drumbeat mixed with horns. Locke stood facing them, giving Haley a blatant once-over before watching Rem with calculating eyes.

A servant offered Haley a glass of wine. She took it and had to stop herself from thanking the dark-skinned woman in English. *"Merci."*

Rem moved closer to Locke, stopping at a chair to pull it back and look at her. She took the silent offer and sat. Locke sat to her right and Rem to her left. Two servants went to work putting lunch before them. A light fare of colorful fruit and artfully prepared fish.

Locke was no longer wearing sunglasses, and Haley had to subdue a shiver when she looked into his chilling, dark eyes.

"I am at a disadvantage," Locke said to Rem. "You said this meeting was important, but you neglected to specify the subject matter."

"It was good of you to invite me," Rem answered, and she heard the edge in his voice, the unspoken taunt.

"As I recall, you left me no recourse. Now, please, do tell me what has brought you all the way here, Rem."

Haley saw the subtle change in Rem, the darkening of his eyes. It showed her just how fervent his desire was for revenge. Cool and calculating. Sure of the end result. She marveled a moment on it.

"This is just a casual visit between old friends," he said, but it was clear it was anything but that.

"Friends." Locke grunted. "I can't recall a time that I didn't feel like looking over my shoulder to see where you were. You were always so different than Dane."

"We never had a chance to get to know each other well."

"You're a hard man to trust."

Rem didn't respond to that. Instead, he said, "I saw you meet with Ammar Farid Salloum."

"Who?"

"No need to deny it. I have pictures."

Locke only stared at him.

"It's interesting, isn't it, that Ammar has been meeting with Habib Maalouf?" Rem continued.

"You talk in riddles."

"Secrets like that can be dangerous," Rem went on, as though Locke hadn't spoken.

"I am keeping secrets now?" He chuckled without humor.

"You'd rather it got out that you've been meeting with a high-ranking operative from Hezbollah who happens to have relations with a diamond merchant?"

Again Locke said nothing, only looked steadily at Rem.

"Some people would think you're helping terrorists launder money by feeding them diamonds," Rem said. "A lot of diamonds. So many that it would be hard for more than the Sierra Leone government to ignore. News like that would travel seas."

Haley covered her surprise. Why was Rem revealing his knowledge of the diamonds? His boldness shocked her. Would they search their bags? Maybe not yet. But after this meeting...

"You're making an assumption that I am not sure I appreciate."

"I'm not assuming a damn thing."

She watched the truth of that waver Locke's confidence.

"What do you want?" he finally asked. "Tell me why you're here."

"I want you to tell me where Ammar's father is."

"His father." Locke sounded incredulous. So was Haley. Why did Rem want to know about Ammar's father?

"Tell me or I'll make sure all the right people know what you're doing with your diamonds."

"You dare to threaten me?"

"What I want is simple."

Long seconds passed. Locke's gaze held firm with Rem's. "I don't know where Farid is," he relented. "He stays hidden because of his rising notoriety with American officials."

Haley got the feeling that revealing this didn't put him in any danger. It wasn't much. The only thing he gave away was the fact that he did, in fact, know Ammar's father. A man named Farid. She glanced at Rem. What other discoveries about him and his past lay in store for her?

"That's why I need you to help me find him," Rem said.

Locke grunted again, more derisively this time. "Even if I knew how to find him, telling you would secure my death."

"Give me something. Anything."

"You've wasted your time coming here."

"Not the way I see it. You may decide not to give me the information I need, but I know of a reporter who'd love to see the pictures I have of you with Ammar." He paused. "And then there are the diamonds…"

Heavy silence ensued.

Locke blinked once. Again. "What diamonds?"

Rem smiled.

More silence hovered, until Locke shifted in his chair.

"He has a ranch in Argentina," he finally said. "In Foz do Iguacu. Perhaps you can learn something there."

"You're going to have to do better than that. He left there as soon as our government started looking for him."

"It's all I know."

Or all he could say, Haley thought.

Rem leaned back in his chair and put his elbow on its arm, resting his head against his forefinger and thumb.

Locke moved his gaze from Rem to Haley and observed her for a moment. She inwardly stiffened with the blatant disregard for her as a person. He looked at her as though she were a slab of pink meat on the other side of a deli counter window. And he hadn't eaten in three days.

"She's not like your other women," he said in English, and Haley wondered if it was an attempt to divert Rem's attention.

"You're right. You haven't slept with her," Rem answered, and Haley nearly lost her poker face.

Locke grinned and resumed his blatant study.

"What do you do?" he asked in French.

What was he asking?

"Her father was into oil," Rem said in French.

Jerking her gaze to him, she was glad she didn't have to cover her surprise that he knew so much about her. When had he discovered that? And how?

"She doesn't have to work," Rem added.

It was true enough. Her mother had died not long after her father had passed at the age of sixty-five. Sometimes she wondered if coming home from Iraq would have been easier if she had family to welcome her instead of a throng of strangers.

"How did you find her?" Locke asked.

"I followed her," Rem said.

Haley wanted to smile at his sarcasm. He *had* followed her.

"We were both on a beach in the Caribbean," he added.

Ah, finally the lie.

"And so you decided to bring her to Monrovia?"

"I have a villa there."

"Still…not the ideal location for an affair. The beaches may look pristine, but they are nothing more than a sewage drain."

"I have business here. You know that."

"Yes. And your business is going to get you killed some day."

"Tell me where Farid is."

Locke didn't respond, but a sly smile inched up the corners of his mouth and he dragged his gaze back to Haley. "I think you lie about this one, Rem."

"I don't care what you think. I don't care what anyone thinks."

True.

"You never did."

"I'll be visiting my reporter friend in a few days. There are people all over the world who're real interested to learn what you're up to. If you think you can hide your involvement with Farid from them, I wish you luck." He unfolded his impressive height and stood, reaching his hand toward Haley.

She realized he'd switched to English and took his hand.

Standing, she saw the dangerous gleam in his eyes. Locke knew how to find Farid but he wasn't going to tell them.

"Be careful, Rem. You're one man against many."

"It's always been that way for me."

Haley found that intriguing. He was resigned to the fact… but also very certain.

A cell phone rang.

Haley watched Locke pull one from his shirt pocket and lift it to his ear. As he listened, his eyes moved from her to Rem but revealed nothing of what the call was about.

"Did he tell you anything?" he asked into the phone. Then after a pause, "All right, I'll be waiting for you." With that he closed the phone and tucked it back into his pocket.

Resting his hand on the table, he looked up at Rem with a sort of resigned coldness. "Your timing is impeccable. I'll give you that."

Rem's smile said his timing had been deliberate.

"Habib was run off the road today," Locke said. "Apparently he was on his way to deliver some diamonds to a client when a white SUV drove alongside him. He was knocked unconscious in the crash, but the man in the SUV stole the diamonds."

"Who was the client?" Rem asked, satisfaction radiating off him. "And why was he calling you?"

Locke's expression hadn't changed. "He wanted to know if I've seen you."

"You didn't tell him."

"Was it you?"

Rem said nothing.

Locke grunted a short laugh. "I wasn't surprised you knew about the diamonds, but I never would have guessed you'd be stupid enough to take them. You're as good as dead. You know that, don't you?" He laughed longer this time. "I don't have to do a thing."

"What's Ammar planning to do with the money he gets from selling the diamonds?" Rem asked.

"How should I know?"

"I think you do."

"You think wrong, my friend."

"How much are they paying you to help them?"

"I sold diamonds to a merchant. It's only business."

"A merchant who's working for Ammar."

Anger brewed in Locke's eyes. "You've got balls coming here."

Haley agreed. How had he known Locke wouldn't kill them the minute he discovered who'd taken the diamonds? He couldn't have. It was a risk, but one he wasn't afraid to take. Even with Haley along.

"Where are the diamonds?" Locke asked.

Rem didn't tell him and Locke looked past them at the two guards standing near the patio door. "Escort these two to their room and make sure they don't come out."

Haley leaned closer to Rem, not liking her fear but unable to control it. He slid his arm around her waist as the guards herded them toward the hall.

"Sleep well," Locke called to their backs, and Haley looked behind her. Between the two guards she saw him smiling wickedly.

Rem closed the door in front of the guards and Haley was glad to see they couldn't be locked inside the room. Not that it mattered, since they still had to get past two armed guards.

She rounded on Rem. "You knew he was going to find out."

He glanced at her but said nothing.

"Why did you risk it?" she demanded. "You're not the only one in this now."

That got his attention. His gaze stayed on her this time.

"You heard him. He doesn't have to do anything. He'll leave that up to Ammar."

"Yes, and he'll keep us here until Ammar arrives." That's why he hadn't bothered searching them. He knew Rem had the diamonds and would let Ammar take them as planned.

"We aren't staying here."

"There are two guards outside the door."

Turning to the bed, Rem opened the duffel containing the diamonds and pulled out his gun. Then he approached her, taking her hand and leading her to the door.

"What are you going to do? Shoot our way out of here?"

"Stand here." He guided her so she leaned her back against the wall a few feet from the door.

Weird, how she believed he actually *could* shoot their way out of here.

"Wait." If he thought she was going to let him do that by himself, he was wrong. She pushed off the wall to go to the bed. Digging in Rem's duffel bag, she found her P99 and returned to the door, leaning right where Rem had wanted her.

He looked from her gun to her eyes and then kissed her once before leaning his back against the wall beside the door, standing next to her. He turned the knob and swung the door open, firing as he moved into the opening. The first silent shot caught the guards unprepared. Haley heard one of them fall. The second got a loud shot off before Rem dropped him.

He ran back into the room to grab his duffel and then took her hand. "Come on!" He pulled her down the hall.

It wouldn't be long before a horde of other guards came after them. They made it almost to the patio door before more gunshots exploded. Outside, Rem hauled her after him, away from the building.

Oh, God. They'd never make it to the helicopter. She spotted more guards running toward them. She aimed her P99 and fired, sending the guards ducking for cover. But the reprieve didn't last. Shots pinged around her. Rem pulled her close to trees but they had to break away in the clearing where the helicopter sat.

Haley dared a glance behind her. A man aimed his gun. Rem shot him and he fell.

At the chopper, he yanked the pod door open and lifted her, throwing her inside and jumping in behind her. She skinned her knees. Bullets clinked and clanged against the door as he slid it nearly shut. Keeping his gun through the opening, he dropped three more guards.

While he shoved his gun in the waist of his pants and rushed to the pilot's seat, she sat in the seat beside him, still gripping her gun. Roughly ten more guards ran toward them, clearing the trees. The rotor revved to flight readiness and Rem lifted the chopper into the air, turning it away from the running guards.

Bullets pinged and banged but faded as Rem flew the bird high into the air.

Haley let her head fall back against the passenger seat and grew aware of her parched mouth, heavy breathing and flying pulse. She felt sick. She was shaking.

"Are you all right?" Rem asked. He didn't even look fazed.

"Yes."

"You're not shot?"

"No." But she did a quick check over her body to be sure. "No."

No thanks to him. She took a few moments to catch her breath and waited for her pulse to slow.

The tiny village came into view, a small break in the thick vegetation. Rem landed the chopper and retrieved the duffel that now contained both of their weapons.

"Are we going to stay here for a while?" Haley asked, as she walked beside him away from the helicopter.

"No."

"What are we going to do?"

"I need to meet with Habib."

What? "You want to go back to Monrovia?"

He didn't answer.

"Ammar will be looking for us. Isn't it kind of stupid to go there? What, are we going back to your villa?"

"We'll be safe there. I need to meet with Habib, and he's in Monrovia."

Was he crazy? "One guard at the gate isn't going to stop a man like Ammar."

"I won't need the guard. In fact, I won't even risk having him there. I'll just lock it down until I'm ready to move."

"So it's you and me against Ammar and his men." Comforting. She shook her head.

"If things go my way, we'll be the only ones there tonight."

"Right. And so far things have gone *exactly* the way you planned." She met his sidelong glance.

"Everything except you."

Chapter 6

The guard at Rem's villa opened the iron gate when they approached. Haley looked around her, up one end of the street and then the other just before Rem drove the Jeep inside the walled area surrounding the villa. She faced forward and was reminded of the grandeur in such an impoverished city.

When he parked, she got out and headed for the front door. Rem stopped her when she reached it. She let him go in before her, watching him pull out his gun. He checked the back patio door and then all the windows on the lower level. She waited for him to come back down from upstairs.

He tucked his gun into the front of his pants and came to stand in front of her.

"All clear?"

Before he could respond, Haley caught sight of movement from the front entrance. She hadn't shut the door. A man entered.

Haley sucked air into her lungs and instinctively reached for the gun that wasn't there. She stepped back. Then froze when she recognized the giant of a man aiming a pistol at Rem.

Calm as ever, Rem stepped the rest of the way down the

stairs and came to a stop in front of Cullen. "How did you get through the gate?"

"I have my ways."

"I'll have to remember to be more careful in the future."

"The good ones always do."

Rem smirked.

"I don't like it when I don't know where my operatives are," Cullen said.

Haley heard the displeasure in his tone. But she didn't need that to tell her he was on the edge. He'd come all the way to Monrovia himself. He hadn't sent any other operatives. That meant one thing.

Rem might get himself killed tonight.

"Cullen."

His gaze shifted to her.

"Wait."

"This has gone on long enough, Haley. It's time for you to go home."

"This involves more than Ammar." She didn't know how else to tell him that Rem knew something and she wanted to find out what it was. "We could stop a much bigger cell than any of us expected coming into this."

"Then I'll send a team to finish it."

"That isn't necessary," she said. "I can do this, Cullen."

"You can't. You think you can, but you can't."

"You underestimate me. You listen to Travis too much."

Travis.

The reminder of him stopped her. "How is he?"

"Under lock and key. If he could get away from his hospital room, he would come after you." She saw the meaning in his eyes. "It's one of the reasons I came here myself. Travis trusts me to bring you home."

She half-smiled at that. It was true. Travis wouldn't trust

anyone else. She could well understand how difficult it must be keeping him sedentary.

"He must be all right, then," she said.

Cullen responded with a slight smile himself. "He's going to be fine, no thanks to you."

Her smile fled. "Hey…"

"You're coming home with me, Haley. No more arguing." He turned to Rem and extended his free hand. "Give me your weapon."

Rem slowly slid his pistol from his pants.

Cullen took it and stuffed it in his own jeans. Then he motioned with his gun for Rem to move into the kitchen.

With a glance at Haley, Rem walked to a kitchen chair and sat. Haley wondered if he was cooperating for her. She doubted Cullen's gun intimidated him much, certainly not enough to stop him from trying to fight his way free.

Cullen lowered his pistol to his side, finger still on the trigger. He must have picked up on Rem's body language, too. Rem wasn't going to fight him.

"I know about your sister," Cullen finally said. "I'm sorry."

Rem's eyes remained steady.

"You worked for Dane Charter, didn't you?"

Now Rem's eyes flickered with emotion, as if he hated his ties to someone like Dane but there was nothing he could do about it. He'd spent so many years living under the perception that he was a man like Dane, he had stopped trying to correct anyone. He expected people to think that way about him. What he didn't see was that he could change the perception if he wanted to. He could have a reputation like Cullen's.

"What happened to make you quit?" Cullen asked.

Why did Cullen ask a question like that? It had nothing to do with Ammar. Or did it?

"Dane was moving drugs for Ammar," Cullen said. "Is that it?"

And Haley grew immensely more interested. It didn't surprise her that Cullen had uncovered Dane's background, but she hoped he could get Rem to reveal more about his involvement with Dane and the connection to Ammar.

"One of his many talents," Rem said, sounding bitter.

"Except his last deal didn't go through," Cullen said. "Know anything about that?"

Rem merely continued to meet Cullen's gaze, a clear sign he wasn't talking, which made Haley wonder what he had to hide.

"It happened right before your sister was killed," Cullen said. "Are the two related?"

Haley looked sharply at him. Why did he think Rem's sister's murder was related to a drug deal? She turned her attention to Rem. She'd wondered why he'd been so vague about his sister's murder. What was he hiding? Apparently Cullen wanted to know the same thing.

"You knew Dane was buying drugs from Ammar," she said, drawing Rem's gaze to her.

He didn't respond and she realized he was wondering if she'd turn out no different than anyone else who assumed things about him based on his past. Was that why he refused to tell her everything about his ties with Ammar?

"Of course he knows," Cullen said, looking at Rem. "You were on the trip to Argentina when Dane brought a load back with him."

Rem's eyes shifted from her to Cullen. "How did you know that?"

"What I'd like to know," Cullen went on, as though he hadn't spoken, "is what happened to the drugs after you made it home. Dane never sold them and he never paid Ammar. It's no stretch to assume Ammar killed him for nonpayment, but where are the drugs?"

"Who told you all this?" Rem demanded.

"One of your mercs decided it was smarter to talk than eat one of my bullets."

"*My* mercs?"

"Charter Security is yours now, isn't it?"

Haley couldn't believe what she was hearing. Then again, maybe she could. Of course, it all fit. His tough childhood had led right into a life of crime. Why not continue along the same path? Flourish, even. Running a rogue private military company.

"Except now it's called Pioneer Security Consultants. Interesting name, given the kind of work you do."

Haley's heart fluttered when Rem's eyes moved to her for a brief glance. Did he care what she thought of this?

"You rented a new building and offered Dane's mercs new jobs," Cullen went on. "Or should I call them *consultants?*"

"Not all of them came to work for me," Rem told him.

Cullen grinned. "I noticed."

Haley couldn't stop staring at Rem. He'd taken over a disreputable private military company, but had he gotten rid of the bad mercenaries and only kept the good? Is that what he meant by "not all of them came to work for me?" The revelation filled her with hope despite her instinct not to let it. He might seem to operate like an honorable man, but he had no ambition to change his reputation. In fact, he seemed to thrive on it, on the power that came with it. No laws applied to him, and he was beholden to no one.

And now there was the mystery of the drug deal that had gotten his ex-employer killed. How much did he really know about that and how did it relate to his sister's death? He wasn't going to tell them. And why not? He didn't care what anyone thought of him, so why not reveal the truth? The answer to both questions couldn't be flattering. More crime to keep his reputation tarnished. His reluctance to tell them bothered her because it only served to support her suspicion.

Maybe the truth threatened him in a way that would cost him too much. With the thought came a chill. That had to be it. Rem wouldn't hide anything about himself for any other reason.

"Did you have anything to do with Dane's drug deal that fell through?" Cullen asked.

"No."

Haley could see nothing in Rem's face that said he was lying. Cullen seemed to be looking for the same signs.

"Did your sister know about it?"

"No."

Again, nothing revealing crossed Rem's expression.

"Help me out here," Cullen said. "There's something I'm missing. You kill someone for raping a woman and Ammar goes after your sister instead of you. Why not just kill you before you left Argentina?"

"Why don't you ask him that?"

"I'm asking you."

Rem remained silent. Until at last he said, "He did try to kill me in Argentina."

And when that failed, Ammar had gone after his sister. That was what Rem wanted her and Cullen to believe. She glanced at Cullen and saw his contemplation. He didn't believe it, either. There was more, but Rem wasn't talking.

"Which side will you be standing on when the rest of what you aren't saying comes out?" Cullen asked. "Mine or Dane's?"

"My own side," Rem answered, his tone as hard as his eyes with the question.

Haley absorbed the power of his conviction along with Cullen. There was something appealing about a man who was so sure of himself that he would join no forces other than his own.

Cullen slid the pistol from his jeans and handed it to Rem. The gesture told her he'd drawn the same conclusion as her. Rem warily took the weapon while Cullen put his own gun into the waist of his jeans.

"Good luck," Cullen said, and turned to Haley. "We'll leave in the morning." To Rem he said, "I'll send you a team."

"I don't need any help."

"I wasn't asking."

Rem's eyes narrowed.

"I'm staying," Haley interrupted the argument that was sure to come. She wanted to find out what Rem was keeping from them. She also wasn't ready to leave Rem. Maybe it was whatever was stirring between them. Maybe it was her own need to shed her past by fighting back.

Cullen shot her an incredulous look. "Don't be ridiculous. You accomplished your mission. You uncovered Habib's connection to Ammar. Now it's time for someone else to step in, and if that someone is Rem, then so be it."

"I wouldn't let anything happen to her," Rem said.

And Haley wondered if he wanted her to stay with him.

"You would do your best not to, but your best may not be good enough. You're dealing with some pretty connected terrorists, and you're only one man."

Rem moved his gaze to her. She felt him wait for her decision. He was sure he could keep her safe, but he also knew she'd be safe with Cullen. That was why he hadn't fought the issue. He'd let her go with Cullen, but he wanted her to stay with him. She was afraid to find out why.

She faced Cullen. "This isn't over."

"It is for you."

"No."

Cullen sighed heavily. "You're too stubborn."

"I can do this," she said.

"You haven't stopped fighting since you came to work for me. I'm afraid it's for the wrong reason. You think if you fight, you can beat what happened to you."

She shook her head. "No." It wasn't the only reason. "It's more than that."

Fighting back had its appeal. She felt invigorated when a mission came to a successful end, when one more bad guy was stopped or killed. She didn't admit to anyone that sometimes the faces of her attackers crossed her mind in those moments. And they were the only moments when she felt at peace, when the horror of it didn't overwhelm her. She felt in charge. Untouchable by her memory's crushing grip.

But now there was Rem. Something about him kept her from leaving. What he was hiding. And him. Something about him compelled her to stay. She ignored her trepidation that whatever she found out about him would dispel any hope that underneath his mercenary shell was a heroic man.

"Be straight with me Haley. If I let you do this, will it help you get over Iraq?" Cullen asked.

Pulled from her thoughts, she answered honestly. "I don't know."

"But you want to try."

She nodded. "Yes."

He studied her. Long seconds passed. "All right. But when you get home, no more missions."

"What?"

"You heard me. This is it. Odie's getting married and put in her notice. I need someone to take her place. I want that person to be you, Haley. No more running around the globe throwing yourself into dangerous situations just so you can prove to yourself you're not a victim."

"She's really going to go through with that, huh?"

Cullen laughed once. "Yeah. She thinks she finally found someone strong enough to handle her."

"I don't know if *strong* is the right word. *Nerdy,* maybe."

Cullen nodded. "It does seem a little off."

"I wouldn't be surprised if she changed her mind and came back to work for you."

"It's definitely not going to be the same without her." Cullen turned to Rem and gestured with his thumb toward Haley. "If she comes home with so much as a scratch, I'm coming after you."

"Then I'm lucky it won't come to that."

Talking Cullen out of one of his decisions was never an easy feat. That she'd done it amazed her and warmed her. He wanted her to overcome her ordeal, and if fighting back would do that, he was going to let her. But only because Rem would be there to protect her.

She wisely didn't mention that Rem had stolen diamonds from Ammar. A whole deadly heap of them. That would surely send Cullen over the edge, and there would be no talking him out of bringing her home.

Chapter 7

Rem handed Haley her Walther P99 and noticed her questioning look. He ignored her. She was the reason he'd gotten next to no sleep last night. That look on her face when Cullen had questioned him kept running through his mind. The way her eyes told truths he didn't want to see.

She was making him care too much. She wondered about his company, and he hated how that gnawed at him. What did she think? Did she question his reasons for taking over and reviving a rogue private military company? His knowledge of Dane's drug dealing with Ammar was enough to raise anyone's suspicion, too. Ordinarily he wouldn't waste much energy worrying about what anyone thought. But with Haley, somehow it mattered.

Sometimes he saw her wavering, as though she were trying to convince herself that he wasn't what he was. A mercenary. Good or bad, that was what he was. Yet, she'd stayed with him. He couldn't allow himself to believe it was for any other reason than to find out what he was sure she thought he was hiding.

He opened the passenger door of the Jeep and closed it after she climbed in. Then he went to the guard shack, which was empty, and checked the street on the other side of the gate. There was a dark car parked about a hundred yards down. Two, maybe three inside.

He'd have to lose them before he called Habib.

Pressing the control to open the gate, he ran back to the Jeep and pulled outside the gate. It would automatically close behind them. The dark car down the street began to move forward.

Rem drove away from the villa compound, then made a turn that took him across United Nations Drive. Haley must have noticed the car, because she had her gun ready and she twisted around to watch it.

On Randall Street, Rem found a side street and squealed tires making the turn. Two more turns and Rem lost the tail. He drove down Benson Street to United Nations Drive. Watching the rearview mirror, he pulled out his satellite phone and called Habib's number.

"You are late," Habib said, when he answered. "You should have called yesterday."

"Something came up." He glanced at Haley and saw her questioning expression. She didn't know whom he was calling, or why, but she would. Soon.

"Is it safe to meet?" Habib asked.

"Yes. Meet me where we planned in thirty minutes."

"I'll be there."

Rem dropped the phone onto the backseat and made a point not to look at Haley again. She was probably steaming mad right now. He'd planned to meet someone and hadn't told her. He hadn't told Cullen, either. She had to be wondering why. After a while, he couldn't resist a quick look. Sure enough, her eyes fired invisible daggers at him. And it irked him to realize he liked that about her. Her fire.

He turned toward the road again.

"Who was that?" she asked. More like demanded. "Who are you going to meet?"

"Habib," he answered. No point in delaying anymore.

"Habib."

He heard the fury in her tone. Mouth slightly parted, eyes beaming anger and disbelief, she was a stunning picture.

"Don't make me ask," she warned.

"What do you want to know?"

"You planned this all along."

Carefully. Very carefully. But he didn't tell her that. "Habib agreed to help me. I couldn't say anything because that would have put him in too much danger. And I needed him."

"He knew you were going to run him off the road?"

"No. He thought we were going to meet somewhere, but I didn't want to risk that. I had to make it look real to Ammar. So that he wouldn't suspect Habib."

He felt her staring at him. "I don't understand. Why did Habib agree to help you?"

"Ammar has been threatening him for years. He's afraid for his family in Lebanon. It's the only reason he's done as Ammar has asked up until now."

"Until he meets you. A man who, what…promises to lift the burden of Ammar all by himself?"

Rem looked at her. Didn't she think he could? Or was there something else she was getting at? "He's tired of living with Ammar constantly breathing down his neck. He wants to end it."

"He must want it to end if he's willing to risk his life and the lives of his family…for you."

Yep, she was getting at something. She knew there was more that he wasn't saying. He just kept driving.

"How will giving you the diamonds help Habib?" she pressed.

"It stops Ammar from using them to forward his cause."

"Yeah, but it also pisses him off."

"He wouldn't harm Habib. He needs a diamond merchant, especially one he can control. Besides, for all Ammar knows, it was me who took the diamonds. He thinks Habib wouldn't try anything like that."

"Why did you want the diamonds?" she asked.

"You'd rather I let Ammar have them?"

"Of course not."

"They'll go a long way to funding my company," he said. And just as he expected, she fell silent. The diamonds would fund his private military company, one that began its operations illegitimately. He could feel her struggle with that. Diamonds taken from the hands of terrorists now would benefit a bunch of lawless mercs.

He grunted a laugh.

"Something's funny about that?" she asked, a bite in her tone.

He shook his head. "You're so predictable."

"I'm predictable."

The sass in her tone made a smile touch his mouth. "Don't worry, I'm used to it."

"To what? People thinking the worst of you?"

"Is that what you're thinking? The worst?"

She turned her head and stared out the side of the Jeep, saying nothing. Just as well. What she knew about him only scratched the surface. If she ever learned all of it, the worst of what she thought would take on a whole new dimension. No point in trying to convince her he was something he wasn't.

Driving into a run-down neighborhood, he parked in front of a small, metal-roofed concrete building that had once been painted white.

Haley got out and walked with him to the door. It opened before they reached it and Habib stepped aside to let them in.

"Did anyone see you come here?" Rem asked.

Habib shook his head and scanned the front of the shack before closing the door. "No one saw." He turned and faced them. "What did you learn from Mr. Merchant?" he asked.

"Nothing. He wouldn't talk. And Ammar called before I could persuade him. Haley and I had to leave in a hurry."

That bit of news appeared to frighten Habib. "So now Ammar will come after you, and you are no closer to finding Farid than you were before."

Rem said nothing.

"You promised," Habib said.

"You have nothing to worry about. He won't hurt you," Rem said, wanting to alleviate his fear. "He needs you too much."

"What am I to do now?" Habib asked anyway. "I risk much doing as Ammar asks. I worry for my family. I am a peaceful man who is content to run his market. What am I to do if he learns of my acquaintance with you?"

"He won't. I'll see to that."

Rem caught Haley's dubious glance and irritation brewed in him. Why did she doubt him? Or was it merely that she doubted he could do this on his own? Take on Ammar alone?

Her attention returned to Habib. "How did you meet Rem?"

He looked surprised by her question. "He came to me."

"And you trusted him?"

Habib smiled almost apologetically with a brief glance at Rem. "I did not at first. But his knowledge of Ammar and his network of contacts soon became apparent to me. That and… well…his background."

Rem watched her eyes move to check his face for anything revealing. What did she want to find? Affirmation? Proof that her instinct about him was right? Which one? The one that painted him a good guy in disguise or the one everyone else saw?

"He promised to rid me of Ammar in exchange for

the diamonds," Habib continued. "To me, it was a worthy trade."

"Yes," she said without breaking their gazes. "I can see how you'd think so."

Rem cocked his head, wondering what she meant.

She just smiled a little and returned her attention to Habib. "Where did Ammar get the money for the diamonds?"

Would she never stop amazing him? Now where was she going with that question?

"I do not know."

"Was Farid in on it?"

"I would assume so, but I cannot be certain."

"Do you think he used a *hawala* broker? Do you know of any that Ammar has been in contact with? That he's used on previous deals?"

Rem folded his arms and waited. Clever girl. He knew she was smart but this was unexpected, even to him.

Habib appeared reluctant to respond.

"Answer the lady," Rem said.

"Yes," Habib said reluctantly.

"Who? Which *hawaladar* does Ammar use to get the money for his diamond purchases?"

Habib glanced uncertainly from Rem to her. "I do not know. *Hawala* brokers are bankers who do not keep detailed records of financial transactions. They work on an honor system. If a man betrays one of his fellow contacts, the price is often death. It is a close-knit network and very difficult to penetrate. Farid may arrange transfers to Ammar from a *hawaladar* near him. That *hawaladar* may contact someone in another country, and that may lead to two or three others, until the chain finally reaches Ammar, wherever he happens to be in the world. But their identities are closely guarded."

"What about couriers? Someone had to have met Ammar

with the money for this last deal. Did Ammar use a courier to transfer the money from a *hawaladar* to him?"

Rem could tell by Habib's subtle blanch that he had. And that only made him more impressed by Haley's well-placed questions. It was obvious that if Farid was hiding out of fear of detection from counterterrorist organizations and governments, he wouldn't use overt channels to get the money to Ammar. But how had she known to ask about a courier? Her background in intel, yes. But she was more experienced than he realized.

He'd have to watch that from here on out.

When Habib didn't answer, Rem turned to him. "What courier did Ammar use?"

The diamond merchant shook his head. "What you ask is too much."

"If you want to rid yourself of Ammar and his men, then tell us where we can find the courier," Haley coaxed. "It will lead us to the *hawaladars* who helped Farid get money to his son. And those *hawaladars* could lead us to Farid himself."

Habib had to know that simply getting rid of Ammar wouldn't solve his problems. Farid had to go, too.

"You assume these *hawaladars* will talk to you. They will not."

"They'll talk," Rem said, and didn't miss Haley's annoyed look.

Eyes heavy with sober thought, the diamond merchant turned his back and wandered to the other side of the dilapidated room. He stopped at a window and stared through the dingy glass.

"Habib—"

Haley held her hand up to stop Rem from pressuring the merchant. He did as she wanted and let her walk to Habib's side.

"No one will know you told us about the courier," she said.

"Ammar will assume Rem found out on his own. He has no reason to suspect you."

"Few know of his courier."

"But Rem has been following Ammar. Isn't it possible he could have seen him with the courier?"

Habib turned his head to look at her.

"You'll have your life back, Habib. But you have to help us. If you know something, please, tell us."

Rubbing his hand down his face with another heavy sigh, Habib's soft brown eyes spoke of the burden he carried. Haley didn't push him, and already Rem could see the diamond merchant softening to her deft manipulation.

"There is a man right here in Monrovia. His name is Charles Henry. That is how Ammar gets his money."

Haley thanked him and Rem took her hand and led her out of the building.

Haley willed her annoyance down to a manageable level as Rem drove outside Monrovia on their way to where Charles lived. Dilapidated buildings painted a desolate picture as they passed. The structures thinned as they left the city. How could she trust him when he kept surprising her with his well-kept secrets? First the diamonds, now Habib.

Cullen hadn't been worried enough to force her to leave Monrovia with him. Why? Was it because he'd decided Rem was one of them? That he believed she was safe with him? It had to be.

That gave her a sinking feeling. If Cullen believed Rem was that trustworthy, it confirmed her assessment of him from the moment they'd met. There was something heroic about him, a trait he didn't appear to see. Still, there was an undeniable dangerous side to him. One that should scare her. Why didn't he scare her?

Well, he did scare her, but not the way she thought he

should. Not from anything stemming from her experience in Iraq.

If she fell for him, she didn't think he had what it took to be with her long-term. His life seemed like such a struggle, like honor was always just out of reach. His actions were honorable, but could he ever get past his bad reputation? Could she? Maybe, if she could ever understand how a man like him had worked his way past her defenses. But she doubted she'd have the chance. Rem would compromise for no one, especially when it came to his reputation. If he didn't think she'd accept him the way he perceived himself, he'd never open his heart to her.

Strange how, prior to Iraq, all the men she'd dated and seen in relationships had absolutely no resemblance to Rem. They'd all been professionals working regular jobs. Fellow soldiers. Ordinary people. Back then, her biggest concern was deciding what she wanted out of the Army. What did she want to do with her life? What kind of man would she marry? All regular, ordinary life issues. Iraq had stripped that innocence from her. And now she was left grappling with a new identity. She didn't know what she wanted from life anymore, much less what kind of man she needed. Did she even need one?

Looking over at Rem, something tickled her insides. She didn't want to feel this way, but a kind of warmth had taken harbor. She didn't understand it and maybe she never would, but no matter what happened between now and when she arrived back home, she would have no regrets. The promise she'd made to herself after Iraq was twofold. She'd never be a victim again. And she'd never look back.

Rem turned a corner and drove to a stop just down the dirt street from a concrete, palm-leaf-roofed shack. Haley was glad for the distraction from her thoughts. She was too tired for them anyway. Red dirt provided the only landscaping. Other small shacks surrounded this one, and thick jungle closed it all in. It was swampy here, so venturing into the trees would be a bad idea if a person didn't know what they were doing.

"We'll wait here until we see him."

She nodded, then snuggled back against the seat and yawned. "Wake me up when you see him." She shut her eyes, rolling her head toward the window so he couldn't watch her sleep.

"Why do you think Cullen left you with me?"

The suddenness of Rem's question made her open her eyes and lift her head to look at him.

"What?"

"He left you. If anything, I would have thought he'd at least stay with us."

"Did you want him to?"

He sent her a "yeah, right" look.

"Maybe he knew I'd be safe with you."

"Is that what you think? That you're safe with me?"

"No," she said, and it was the truth. "I probably would be safer with Cullen."

A harsh breath blew through his nose. "You'd be dead as soon as he left you with someone less competent. And that would be pretty much anybody." Anger nipped his tone.

She ignored it. His ego was showing and she wanted to see where it led. "Except you?"

"I've had lots of practice."

"So has Cullen."

"I wasn't comparing."

She let that go.

"Is he right?" Rem asked.

"About what?"

"The real reason he left you with me. It isn't to gather intel, either."

Because Cullen believed she needed this to overcome Iraq.

That was what he meant. She had to push back her rising defenses.

"Don't do that." She didn't want him to start digging up unwanted memories.

"He sees it as a way to help you heal."

"I don't throw myself into dangerous situations to get over Iraq."

"Then why did you come with me?" His gruff tone exposed his vulnerability to the subject.

And that was why he'd started asking questions. This was what he really wanted to know. Haley could have gone with Cullen. Rem wouldn't have forced her to stay. Not with Cullen in the room. But she had stayed. And now he wanted to know why. Yes, she wanted to uncover his secrets. Yes, she needed to heal from Iraq. But none of that mattered. He wanted to know if she'd come with him for any other reason.

That warmed her core and sent a responding sensation pulsing to the rest of her body. But she couldn't let him think she was starting to have feelings for him. She had to protect her heart.

"To fight terrorism. And win." Unlike she was able to do in Iraq. The thought came against her will.

"You don't have to risk your life to do that."

Was she mistaking the brief look in his eyes before he turned back to the road as disappointment?

"You can fight with your mind, Haley," he said.

"I won't argue that's part of it."

"How did you know to ask Habib about the *hawala* brokers?"

"I know how terrorists think. I know how they operate. It's my job."

"Yes. Intelligence is your job. Not ops. So why put yourself in those situations?"

"I don't go out of my way to do it."

"That's not what I heard Cullen say."

She didn't deny it.

"If he had his way, you'd never leave U.S. soil. You can do intel from there just as well as you can in the field."

"What's your point?" she snapped.

"You were afraid when we reached Locke's compound."

"Who wouldn't be afraid?"

"Why do ops when it's clear that you're not cut out for it?"

It was the fear she wanted to overcome, but she couldn't bring herself to admit that to him.

"You should have never come to Monrovia in the first place."

"Oh, and you're here because you want to make a difference in the world." Her sarcasm stemmed from the emotion he'd roiled to life. She couldn't help it.

But he didn't even flinch. He accepted who he was—who he thought he was, anyway—and he didn't care what anyone else thought.

"I'm here to kill Ammar and his father," he said, a deadly undertone leaving no doubt of his passion on the matter. "No other reason. And nothing. Nobody. Not a single living thing is going to get in my way."

"I understood that from the moment I met you." It was what had fascinated her about him. She knew that now. His energy fascinated her. The vengeful mercenary who denied his hero's heart.

They stared each other down. Haley felt her pulse hammering and saw his pumping in the vein of his neck.

A movement caught her eye. She looked with Rem toward the building. A man rode a motorcycle to a stop in front of the building and climbed off. He strode into the shack.

Rem got out of the Jeep. Haley did, too, and followed him across the street.

Charles glanced back just before he shut the door and paused. His eyes flared wide in recognition before he recovered and started to slam the door shut. Rem reached the door and slapped a hand to stop him.

"You know me," Rem said.

"You must leave here," Charles said in a heavy native accent.

"How do you know me?"

"I do not."

Rem shoved the door, sending Charles stumbling backward as he advanced into the building.

Haley looked in one direction and then the other to make sure no one noticed. Watching a dark-skinned youth buzz by on his motorcycle without seeing them, she followed Rem inside and closed the door. The interior was surprisingly comfortable, given the weathered appearance of the exterior. A framed painting adorned one marginally dirty wall, and the furniture looked relatively new. There was even a portable stereo, which told her Charles must have a generator. A real commodity in this part of the world.

"Tell me how you know me," Rem demanded, advancing forward.

Charles backed away a few more steps and then stopped. It was several seconds before he spoke. "Ammar showed me your picture. He also warned me that you might pay me a visit."

"All I need is the name of the *hawaladar* Ammar used."

Charles grunted a mocking laugh. "It would be suicide for me to tell you that."

"It'll be murder for me if you don't."

Haley shot a look at Rem. Did he mean it? He'd kill this man if he didn't give him the information he sought?

Rem slid his gun from the front of his jeans. Charles watched the movement with uncertain, fearful eyes.

"You must understand," he pleaded, "I can not betray Ammar."

"He doesn't have to know."

"If you go to this *hawaladar* you seek, Ammar will know who told you how to find the man."

"Then maybe it's time for a career change. You can leave the country."

"There will be nowhere to go to escape Ammar."

Haley believed him, and she suspected Rem did, too. But he didn't seem to care.

"You'll tell me or I'll kill you."

"If you kill me you will never learn the identity of the *hawaladar*."

Rem stepped closer, lifting his pistol. He angled the barrel against Charles's temple and slid the metal down the man's face. Reaching the soft skin under Charles's chin, he pressed upward. Charles knocked Rem's wrist with his hand, nearly dislodging the contact. Rem kneed the man, making him bend forward and groan. Rem grabbed some of his shirt and forced him upright again. Charles's eyes were round with fear and his breaths came out in shallow pants. Rem swung the pistol and struck Charles. The man shouted in pain, and blood trickled from a gash on his cheek.

"Rem!" She didn't want to witness a torture.

Her frantic tone didn't seem to faze him.

"The name," Rem demanded, pressing the gun against the man's temple again. "Tell me. Now."

Haley moved over to him and slid her hand over the muscle of his forearm. "Rem."

At last, he acknowledged her, turning his head to meet her eyes.

"Stop this."

She'd never seen such coldness in his eyes before. How many times had he slipped into this fighter? This rebel marauder?

Did he really think violence was the only way he'd get Charles to talk?

"Go outside if you can't handle this, Haley," he said.

That just made her mad. "I will not stand aside while you beat someone up at gunpoint and threaten to kill him."

He lowered the pistol. "Try to run and I will kill you." Then he turned to face her, looming tall above her, anger making the coldness in his eyes that much more menacing.

"Wait outside."

"Go to hell."

One side of his mouth cocked upward. "Already there, sweetheart."

Charles began to sidle away, but Rem lifted his gun and aimed it at his forehead. "Move again and you're a dead man."

The man froze, terrified.

Haley grunted her dismay. "If you kill this man it will be murder, and that's exactly what I will report when I get back to the States."

His gaze held hers for a long moment. "All right," he said. "Give it your best shot." He glanced purposefully at Charles. "See if you can get him to give you a name."

Haley moved closer to Charles, who looked back at her with a mixture of gratitude and wariness.

"Just tell us where we can find him," she said.

He glanced from Rem to her again and didn't say a word.

"We'll stop Ammar. He won't have a chance to hurt you," Haley continued.

But Charles kept his lips shut tight.

"Please," she urged.

Rem sighed and shoved his gun into the waist of his jeans. "You make a real lousy operative, darling."

She sent him a derisive smirk.

He dismissed her and looked around the room. When he

spotted an open doorway, he grabbed a fistful of Charles's shirt and forced the man to precede him into the adjoining room. Haley followed into the bedroom. There was a desk across from the foot of the bed.

Rem pushed Charles so that he sat on the end of the bed. "Don't move."

Charles sat on the bed and didn't try to escape.

Rem faced the desk and began to rummage through papers scattered on the surface. He opened drawers and searched those, too.

Haley caught Charles glancing at the wastebasket beside the desk. He did it more than once. She went to the trash can and knelt there. Sifting through discarded papers, she retrieved a crumpled handwritten note. Only a name and an address were written.

She straightened to see that Rem had stopped his search and now watched her. She handed him the paper.

He took it and read. His eyes lifted.

Haley folded her arms and raised her brow in a silent I-told-you-so. He didn't have to resort to violence to get what he wanted.

Chapter 8

After watching Haley sleep on the flight to South Africa and suffering an attack of affection, Rem was in no mood for her sass. Right now she walked beside him on the way to the front door of their Cape Town hotel, a confident bounce to her steps. The corners of her mouth curved in a subtle smile, as though she sensed the cause of his mood and thought he deserved it.

What was it about her that got to him? Yeah, she was gorgeous with that silky brunette hair and those almond-shaped, tropical sea-blue eyes, but there was more to it than that. Maybe it was the way she seemed to see right through him. Maybe it was her purity. More likely it was her knack for confusing the hell out him.

"Why do you always wear your hair up in a ponytail?" he asked, the words springing on him as a result of his thoughts.

The curve of her mouth flattened and she looked at him. "What do you care?"

"You don't like wearing dresses and you never let your hair down. Why not just shave it off?"

Stopping before they reached the hotel doors, she reached

up and yanked the band from her hair and shook her head. Long, dark, glorious strands spread over her shoulders and down her back. Some hung close to her face, hugging it like the palm of a man's hand. He couldn't see her eyes behind her sunglasses, but he knew they were full of rebellion.

Damn, he wished he would have kept his mouth shut. Instead of pushing her buttons, he'd given her a reason to push his. He wanted to bury his hands in her hair, pull her head back and kiss her.

"Are you one of those types who can't stand to be wrong?" she asked.

Where was she going with that question? "What was I wrong about?"

"What would you have done to that man if we hadn't found the note?"

Of course, she already knew, but he indulged her. Did she think he wouldn't? "Made him talk."

"How?"

"You know how," he said.

"He wouldn't have talked," she countered.

He stopped arguing. What was the point? Around them, people walked past. A man entered the hotel.

"I just don't understand why you keep doing it."

He looked at her. "Doing what? Threatening people for information? It's the only language a lot of them understand."

"No, I mean the whole thing. The profession. And that man was different. He wasn't like Ammar. You threatened an innocent."

"An innocent who delivers money to terrorists." The other part of what she said grated on him. "I do what I have to do."

"Yes, and you're so accepting of it."

Accepting of being a merc. "What else am I supposed to

do? Wait tables? Tend bar?" He grunted his derision. "No thanks."

"You're not looking deep enough. You're in a box. Step outside of it for two seconds and you'll understand what I mean."

"What do you think I would see when I step out of your box, Haley? A way to be heroic in the eyes of all the McQueens of the world?" He let out a sarcastic laugh. "You say I should step outside the box. Well, for the record, I'm already out of it. I've been out of it since I was fourteen years old. So maybe you're the one still stuck inside."

She didn't say anything, which told him he'd given her plenty to think about. Good.

Why were they having this conversation, anyway? He sighed, stepping around her to open the door to the Cape Grace Hotel. He waited for her to enter ahead of him. Leaving the hazy early-evening heat of the busy street, he led her to the reception counter and checked them into a room with two beds. In the elevator, they stood on opposite sides and then she preceded him down the hall.

Holding the room door open for her, he followed her inside. A short hall opened to a bright room with white trim accenting pale green carpet and splashes of red. A wall of windows with French doors opened to a terrace. Haley dumped her duffel on the white comforter of one of the beds.

Rem picked up the hotel phone and ordered room service. It gave him something to do as he covertly noticed her watching him. Try as he might to be unaffected, it was no use. Her attention was as annoying as it was tantalizing. Would she resume her probing, or would she just stand there and turn him on? He didn't want to hurt her, but that was how she would end up if she continued to try and excavate his motives and ideology, which according to her were entirely too sycophantic for his credit.

She sat cross-legged on the bed, doing a poor job of pretending to be immersed in a brochure about the famous diamond pit, the Kimberly Mine. They were driving to Kimberly tomorrow. He moved to the French doors and looked outside. Yachts floated in the harbor. Setting sunlight painted the buildings along the curving shore.

"You're more like Cullen than you think, you know."

He turned. She hadn't even looked up from the brochure, giving her a nonchalant appearance. But there was nothing nonchalant about her comment. When was she going to give this up? "Enough, Haley. Let it go."

"It's the truth."

He moved toward her. "The truth is I made money dealing drugs and then turned my street smarts over to a private military company. I survived. I didn't get where I am today by winning the respect of colonels and comrades." He stopped before her where she sat on the bed. "Why is that so hard for you to accept?"

She put the brochure down beside her and looked up at him. "It doesn't matter how you got where you are now. The point is, you are."

"Don't waste time analyzing me." She wasn't on the right track anyway. He didn't have a problem with himself, despite her penchant for nailing him with one. He liked who he was. He was comfortable in his skin.

Gracefully pushing off the bed, she stood. "Funny how watching you is making me see things about myself."

He was too curious to stop her from continuing. Never mind what her nearness was doing to him. He looked down at her mouth and then back into her eyes, waiting.

"I need to find a way to overcome what happened to me," she said, "and I'm starting to think Cullen and Travis are right. I won't be able to do that working ops."

Her confession took him aback. He didn't want to know why her assessment about him had led her to that conclusion.

"In a way, you're doing the same. You're so immersed in the stigma of your profession that you can't separate it from the man you've become."

"How is that related to your situation?"

"I've been so immersed in putting Iraq behind me that I didn't see what I was doing...putting myself in dangerous situations...fighting back."

"When you can do that from Roaring Creek."

"Yes."

He understood what she meant now, but there was still something she was missing. "I've made peace with the course of my life a long time ago, Haley."

"Maybe that's your problem."

He cocked his head, wishing she'd stop. Just stop.

"Let it go, Rem."

Let what go?

"Let your past go," she said as though reading his thoughts.

What would it take to make her understand? She wasn't going to change him. "I was going to kill that courier."

"No, you weren't."

"Oh, yes, I was."

"I don't believe you."

"You don't want to believe that I'm capable of it."

"No, I know you are capable of it. Of killing. But I also know you need a good and just reason for it."

He felt himself stiffen, resisting what she said. Was she trying to find a way to justify her feelings for him? Her desire for someone like him? Someone she didn't want to feel that way for? Someone who shouldn't give her the conduit she needed to get over her experience in Iraq. Maybe she was trying too hard to turn him into something heroic, something worthy of her love.

Or was she simply more accurate than he wanted to admit?

"And there was none back there," he heard himself say, because that was what she meant.

"No."

God, she'd threaded her way into his heart so expertly he hadn't seen it coming. He'd never known anyone who believed in him the way she did. Understood him. He wondered if she understood him better than he understood himself. Was he so conditioned to hard living that he couldn't recognize what was good anymore? He'd spent too many years crossing the line of morality. Maybe his judgment was blurred.

A knock on the door announced the arrival of room service, and he was never gladder for the distraction.

Waiting for Rem to get back from meeting the *hawaladar* made Haley restless. He'd gone while she slept and it had infuriated her. Until worry had worked its way past that emotion and taken over. What was he doing? Was he all right? What if he was hurt and needed help?

She paced one end of the room to the other, wearing a slinky number he'd packed with the other frilly things in the duffel. Her dark nipples showed through. She'd have to be careful when he returned. Make sure she was in bed and under the covers. But for now, she couldn't unwind enough to sit still, much less lie down.

She stopped at the French doors, gazing out at the yacht marina and Cape Town's enchanting shoreline. Running her hand over the soft material of the nightgown, she marveled that it didn't suffocate her the way these kinds of clothes usually did since Iraq. In fact, she felt a little excited with the prospect of Rem coming back to her when she looked like this.

She didn't understand it, but the more time she spent with him, the more she talked to him, the more she learned about him, the safer she felt with him. The safer she felt to be a woman with him. He didn't know it yet, but he was a good man.

The click of the door made her body jerk. She turned in time to see the object of her thoughts enter.

He froze when he saw her, his hand still on the door handle and the door remaining wide open. He wore a black short-sleeved golf shirt with dark blue jeans and black boots, looking trim and big and sexy. His black hair was thick and messy. Light from the lamps on each side of the bed cast shadows in the short hallway leading to the door. She could see enough of his eyes to know his gaze had dipped to take in her body.

She crossed her arms over her breasts. What was she thinking, fantasizing about him seeing her like this? Had she subconsciously arranged for it to come true?

Appearing to recover from walking into the room to see her wearing next to nothing, he took one step forward and shut the door. He hesitated there, standing just inside the door. She felt the energy of his gaze, felt his building desire. It triggered her own, and that frightened her. Her heart began to hammer. What if he wanted to have sex with her? Was she ready for that? Would she ever be ready to have sex with a man like Rem?

He began to move farther into the room, passing the threshold of the hall and emerging into the light. Her breath stopped as the glow of his eyes took on more detail. When he came to a halt in front of her, she had to catch her breath. Without taking his eyes from the connection with hers, he slid his hands down her folded arms until he reached her hands. Gently, he took them in his and lowered their arms, entwining his fingers with hers and moving closer.

Warm bursts of desire fluttered inside her as she looked up at the growing passion in his eyes.

"Rem?"

"Don't be afraid of me, Haley."

His raspy tone made her close her eyes and dip her head back, turning it slightly to one side, part of her wanting to put distance between them, another wanting him to do whatever he wanted with her. He stepped closer still, his body brushing hers. Her nipples hardened with the erotic contact against his chest.

He dipped his head. She felt his breath on her neck just before he kissed her there. Tingles radiated from the touch. She shivered. Parted her lips to breathe easier.

Yes. Her heart cried. It had been so long. Would he be the one to end the struggle? The turmoil? It seemed so unlikely. *He* seemed so unlikely to be the one. Why him? She didn't understand why it was him who made her yearn for this.

His mouth caressed her skin as he made a path up to her jaw. It was a natural thing for her to turn her head to meet his mouth. He kissed her. A feather-light touch that sent a shimmer of pleasure trickling down to her limbs.

His arm slid around her waist and he pulled her flush against him. He opened his mouth and she gave him everything he asked for. His deep groan sent another shimmer of pleasure through her. Looping her arms around his neck, a sound came up her throat as his other hand curved over her rear. When he discovered her bare underneath, he swore in French.

Oh, no, this was quickly escalating beyond her control. Every time he touched her the flames burned hotter. Still, she threaded her fingers into his hair and angled her mouth to take his tongue deeper.

His hand on her rear tensed. He gripped her flesh and pulled her against his erection.

She had to pull her mouth back and take ragged breaths. Tipping her head back, she kept her eyes closed to sensation.

Rem's hand found its way under the hem of her nightgown. It traveled up the back of her bare thigh, the back of it, came to the curve of her rear. He caressed her there and then slid his long fingers down until they found her soft, warm wetness.

A low, deep growl of a groan rumbled from him. He moved his middle finger between her folds. Haley heard her own ragged breaths. She lifted her knee alongside his hip to give him easier access.

He took the invitation and sank his finger as deep as he could reach. It drew a guttural sound from her. He kissed her through it, his tongue matching what his finger was doing. She came hard. He stilled his finger through the clenching release.

Coherency floated back to her in a fog. She opened her eyes. Rem lifted his head. His breaths puffed against her mouth. His eyes communicated a need that penetrated her. He needed her. Needed to be inside her.

Inside her.

More coherency returned.

He wanted to make love. Put his erection inside her. Images of Iraq assailed her.

She tensed.

He immediately noticed. She saw it in his face. In the way the heat changed from unbridled desire to restraint born of pure willpower.

The muscles in his jaw flexed. He slid his finger out of her and she lowered her leg as he stepped back. He stood there a few seconds, breathing irregular, looking at her nipples and lower before returning to her face.

"I need to go down to the bar for a while," he told her.

And a rush of warm affection for him swarmed her. He understood. She nodded.

He turned and left the room, closing the door with a hard thud.

Leaning her head back, she shut her eyes and immersed herself in the feelings he'd left her with. She rubbed her hands over her body, wishing they were Rem's hands, wishing she hadn't withdrawn. Collapsing on the bed, she rolled onto her back with her arms thrown above her head, looking at the ceiling. This was the closest she'd come to being with a man since Iraq. Would Rem be the man to cure her?

Maybe it would be best if she stayed focused on her purpose here.

Then she remembered he hadn't told her what he'd found from the *hawaladar*.

"Another," Rem said to the bartender when the man came over to check on his drink.

The bartender nodded and poured another scotch.

Someone slinked onto the barstool beside him.

He glanced over. Then looked again.

Haley.

She'd dressed in the white shorts he'd packed for her, along with a low-cut black-and-white top that revealed more of her breasts than he could handle right now.

"You should not have come down here," he said.

She met the meaningful look he sent her with a smile. "Relax, we're in public."

"For now."

She looked down at that before recovering and meeting his gaze again. "What did you find out tonight?"

So she had a reason for daring to be near him. "The name of another *hawaladar*."

"Another?"

"That's how the they work. Someone contacts the first one with instructions on a financial transaction, and that *hawaladar* contacts another to carry it out. Different countries. Different couriers. Very little record keeping."

"I'm aware of how the system works."

"How could I have forgotten?" Maybe it was when he had his finger drenched in her wetness. Yeah, that explained it.

"Rem…"

He noticed her reluctance but didn't feel like helping her.

"About earlier…"

"No need to talk about it," he said. God, please, don't make her want to talk about that now.

"I—"

"Haley."

"I wanted to—"

"It's okay, really."

"No. I wanted to…you know."

"Yeah. I know."

"Make love," she said anyway.

He started to get aroused. "I get it. No problem."

"No. I mean…"

He sensed her need to talk and struggled with his physical reaction. Did she know how badly he wanted to get her naked?

"I—I…i-it's just that it's…"

Rem swiveled his bar stool and took her hands in his. She glanced down and then back up into his eyes, spearing him even more with emotion he couldn't fight.

"Don't talk about this, Haley. Please." He was afraid he sounded desperate. Had he ever felt like this before? He didn't think so. "I understand. There's no need to explain it to me."

"But—"

"If you keep talking about it, I'm not going to be able to stop myself from taking you back up to the room and spending the rest of the night wiping out every bad memory you have of Iraq." He said it as gently as he could.

Her head jerked back a bit and her mouth formed an O.

"Can I get you anything?" the bartender asked.

Rem was glad for the interruption.

Haley turned an awkward gaze to the man. "I'll have what he's having." ·

Chapter 9

After landing in Prague, Haley wished they'd come for a vacation instead of locating another globe-trotting *hawaladar*. She hadn't asked how Rem had gotten the information from the last one and she didn't want to know.

She rode with Rem in a taxi along crowded streets lined with ancient buildings. She couldn't absorb enough of the beauty that passed her window. The taxi came to a stop in front of the Prague Marriott Hotel. The *hawaladar* Rem had located ran a boutique in Wenceslas Square, a short ride from here.

Inside, the spacious lobby was beige with accents of maroon and black. Crystal fountains showcased an already grand staircase. Haley waited while Rem checked in, then rode the elevator with him. He hadn't said when they'd meet the second *hawaladar*. It was early afternoon and she was hungry. They'd skipped lunch. The prospect of dinner with Rem gave her stomach a noticeable case of butterflies. She wondered if he'd want room service again. In Prague? Even as uneasy as she felt spending what could be construed as intimate moments if they stayed in the room, she couldn't waste an opportunity to get out and explore an exotic city.

She'd read on the way here there were some good restaurants on Parizska Street. Along with some upscale shops. Cartier, Gucci, Louis Vuitton, Hermès Paris, Christian Dior. They were all there. Not that she was interested in going into any of them. At her rising ambivalence Haley slowed her steps on her way into the room. Did she want to go shopping?

Wandering into the room, vaguely noticing the rich hues of maroon and cream, she sat on a cream-colored chair. She hadn't wanted to do that since before Iraq. There were a lot of things she did before Iraq that didn't have the same appeal now. Shopping made her feel feminine, which usually reminded her how vulnerable she was as a woman. And that always led to thoughts of her ordeal, threatening to unearth memories she needed to keep buried. It was a constant fear. That one day something would trigger a horrible memory that would unleash a blow-by-blow replay of what had happened to her. The best she could hope for was that she had gone unconscious before the worst of what the doctors had said her body had suffered.

Rem glanced at her as he put a duffel on the king-sized bed. Glanced again. Of course, he'd notice a change in her. She doubted if he ever missed anything.

"What's wrong?" he asked.

"Nothing."

She could see his doubt.

She jumped to her feet. "Let's go walk down Parizska Street." Anything to get them out of this room and him from questioning her too much. She didn't have to shop. Just take in the sights. What harm would there be in that?

She walked toward the door, swung it open and looked expectantly back at Rem. Without saying anything, he approached the door. She could barely meet his gaze, it was so astute right now. He knew something had gotten to her.

She hurried ahead of him to the elevator doors. He stopped

beside her where she waited for them to open, feeling him take her in. She ignored him. The elevator doors opened and she stepped inside. He pressed the button for the lobby floor.

At the third floor the elevator stopped and a woman entered. Blond-haired, blue-eyed, tall and slender, she looked first at Rem, then Haley. But her attention returned to Rem and her eyes took on an unmistakable hint of interest. Haley tried to ignore Rem's indifference to it.

The elevator doors opened and the woman left first. Haley left next, ahead of Rem. He put his hand on her lower back as they made their way through the elegant lobby.

Outside the hotel, Rem got a cab. He told the driver where to go and then leaned back against the seat beside her. She took in the sights of old architecture on the short ride to Parizska Street. The cab stopped and they got out.

Shops lined the street, pretty and inviting. A smile burst onto Haley's face.

"Oh," she breathed.

Rem smiled, just enough to let her know he liked her response. "Have you ever been here?"

"No."

"Never? Not even to the Czech Republic?"

"No." He reached his hand toward hers and she automatically gave it to him.

The heat and roughness of his skin stole her focus a moment as she started walking with him. She couldn't keep thinking of that hand running over her bare skin and going between her legs. So she let the grandeur of some of the shops take her mind off of it.

Passing one amazing window display after another, she had to fight the urge to go into one. A boutique displaying a black dress in the window pushed her over the edge. She didn't know why it caught her eyes. It was a dress. Very feminine, very something she would have worn pre-Iraq.

Haley entered the store and drifted between artfully arranged displays of clothes.

She chose a few tops she liked, but the black dress on a mannequin kept nudging her. Searching around the shop, trying to be nonchalant about it, she finally found the dresses. She checked on Rem. He'd found himself a chair near the dressing rooms. Great. Exactly where she didn't want him. Plus, he'd been watching her the way he had when she'd left the hotel room. By now he'd probably put together what this was about. She had issues with her femininity and something was making her overcome it today.

Yes, it was a sign that she was healing from Iraq. But the part Rem played in it made her uneasy. She was afraid she wasn't doing this for herself. That really she wanted to look feminine for *him*. And why? Because she wanted him. But how could she ever have him?

It didn't have to be for the rest of her life. The thought came as she found her size in the black dress. She hesitated before heading for the dressing rooms. What if she just had sex with him? It was another step closer to healing. If he could help her do that, what was wrong with going after him? She went to an area of shoes and found a pair of black sandals before weaving her way to a dressing room.

Inside, she tried on the dress. Something told her it was going to look great. And it did. It flattered her curves without being overly suggestive. Sexy, but nice.

She wanted to wear it. Now. To dinner.

She froze in the act of admiring the drape of material that fell to her knees.

With Rem?

He was in jeans. The dress was pretty casual…

Yes. She wanted to be with him. Intimately. Dinner would be a good start.

Oh, hell. Was she really considering this?

Before the thinking part of her could rationalize it further, she pulled off the tags and slipped into the sandals. Opening the dressing room door, she saw Rem's lifting eyes and quickly averted her gaze. She caught his sort of come-to-attention turn-of-the-head as she passed him on the way to the checkout counter with the clothes she had been wearing.

She handed the clerk the tags from the dress and the empty shoe box and realized she didn't have any money. All her things were in Rem's duffel bag. Rem appeared beside her, wallet already open. He dropped money and the clerk bagged her things, eyeing her and then Rem.

"What's this all about, Haley?" he asked, as they left the shop.

"I might never get to Prague again. It'll be nice to have something to take home with me."

"You know that's not why you're wearing that dress."

"I'm hungry. I want to go somewhere for dinner."

"You could barely wear that sundress at Locke's compound."

"But I did wear it."

Without arguing further, he reached for her hand again, the rougher skin of his sliding over hers as their fingers laced. However sweet and innocent the contact was, it sent a tingle of delight sparkling through her.

The sun had set, and the lights along Parizska Street cast the old architecture in spectacular detail.

Rem led her down the street a block and a half before coming to Pravda. Through the window she could see candlelit white tablecloths. People were dressed in everything from jeans to evening wear.

She felt the loss of Rem's hand as he held the door open for her. Inside, the detail of the white moldings accented the contemporary decor. A hostess sat them at a row of tables with one long bench seat topped with beige and white pillows.

Brown wicker chairs lined the opposite side of the tables. She chose the bench seat, and Rem sat across from her on a wicker chair.

He ordered wine, and she studied the menu of varied international fare. Chilean sea bass. Tiger prawn wok. Beef tenderloin. It all sounded good to her, so when Rem ordered the sea bass, she ordered the same and then settled back against the seat to look at him.

His gaze caught hers and lowered to the front of the dress before returning. His eyes slowly blinked in recognition of her direct look, and she witnessed his rare softening. She let herself fall into the energy that hummed between them and the way it made her feel to have him look at her like that.

She knew where this night was headed. And it gave her a flash of apprehension. He couldn't be the right man for her. Not with her history. And yet, there was this pull between them.

"This restaurant reminds me of the one our neighbor owned growing up," Haley said from across the table, anything to cool off their chemistry. She looked around the restaurant. "The decor. The smells." She inhaled, closing her eyes and tipping her head back a little, savoring the sensory enjoyment it brought her.

He lifted his glass of wine and leaned back against the chair again. She watched him, unable to deny how much she liked doing that. Just staring at him. At his eyes. She loved his eyes. Especially when they lost their icy indifference, like right now.

"He had a daughter who was a couple of years older than me," she continued, forcing herself to remain focused on their conversation. "We used to play all the time. We'd pretend there was a village in a vacant field behind our house. The field was full of tiny hills and valleys that would fill with water in the spring. We'd put on waders and walk through there, imagining buildings and houses on waterfront property." She smiled and laughed softly. "God, I was so innocent then."

She shook her head, absorbed with the memory.

"You were just a kid," Rem said.

It was more than that. "I had such a good childhood. Stable parents. Lots of friends. The first time anything bad happened to me was when my dad died of cancer eight years ago. My mother died not long after that. She had a massive stroke. It was as if she couldn't live without him."

"Do you have any siblings?"

"No. I was an only child. I suppose that's why I used to have so many friends."

"You don't anymore?"

She smiled. "I work too much."

He didn't return her smile; instead, he studied her. She sensed him adding things up in his mind. That always made her uncomfortable. He saw too much about her.

"I wish I could have saved you from Iraq," he said in a low, intimate tone.

She fell into the way he looked at her, warm emotion stirring.

"Maybe you still can," she said, equally quiet.

As his eyes smoldered, she knew he'd caught her meaning.

The main course arrived, but she'd lost her appetite. Rem hadn't moved to touch his, either. Just kept looking at her, heating her more and more with each second that passed. Without saying anything, he dumped money on the table and stood, moving closer to her and extending his hand, a silent invitation.

She found herself giving him her hand and he led her out of the restaurant. Her heart beat fast while he got them a cab. She climbed into the back and he sat right next to her. His thigh pressed along hers.

He slid his hand over and entwined his fingers with hers. She turned her head to see him. He leaned over and kissed her, a gentle caress. Then he just hovered his mouth over hers, parted his lips, teasing her until she couldn't resist arching to reach him. He kissed her deeply, gave her his tongue. She lost her breath for a second as sensation tickled every nerve ending in her body.

The kiss grew in urgency. His wet lips slid against hers, slipped in an erotic caress. She freed her hand from his and twisted to loop her arms around his neck. He wrapped his arms around her and moved her onto his lap.

Yes.

She felt his hand on the back of her head, holding her firm for his searching tongue. The cab came to a stop but she didn't care. Rem didn't, either, judging by the way his other hand roamed over the curve of her hip and up her ribs.

But he removed his mouth from hers. Their breaths met in the space between their mouths. Want clenched in her abdomen when she opened her eyes to the deep, dark desire in his.

Behind her back, he opened the cab door. Haley turned on his lap so she could get out, but his erection beneath the material of his jeans rubbed between her legs. Rem grunted and she stumbled as she climbed to her feet outside the cab.

Her knees felt unsteady while she waited for him to pay the driver. She didn't want to think about what the driver had seen, much less what he thought.

Rem climbed out of the cab and took her hand, his face set with determination. She let him tug her inside the hotel. She half-trotted to keep up with him. At the bank of elevators, Rem stabbed the Up button. It seemed an eternity before the elevator doors opened. It was empty. He pulled her inside and pressed the button to close the door, then their floor number.

Haley tugged his hand as she moved to lean against the elevator wall. She wanted him against her. Rem sank his fingers into her hair and kissed her. She spread her feet apart on the elevator floor and he moved his hips in answer, swearing in French.

She smiled against his mouth and told him how good he felt in the same language.

"You're so beautiful," he said, still in French. His hands kneaded her rear, pressing her against him.

The elevator doors opened. An old woman stood stiffly in the hall, eyes widening at the sight of them.

Haley hung her head as Rem pulled her behind him out of the elevator and down the hall. She ran her hands up his back as he opened the room door. She felt outside of herself, as if another woman was so brazenly touching this frightening man. She was going into a hotel room with him, where he would make love to her. He would penetrate her. Invade her the way she'd been told she'd been invaded in Iraq. Would it be like that? Her mind told her no, but another part of her couldn't separate the horror from what could have with Rem.

Thinking of it in those terms stopped her. She stepped into the room only enough to allow the door to close. What was she doing?

Rem didn't seem to notice the dose of reality that had just descended upon her. He peeled off his shirt and let it fall to the floor. The sight of his bare chest distracted her. He slid his gun from his pants and put it on the table and stepped out of his shoes. Then he just looked at her, as if waiting for her to do something.

She didn't. Couldn't.

Finally, he noticed the change in her. He moved toward her, those long, strong legs striding cautiously.

Haley couldn't get enough air. She felt more and more suffocated as he approached. When he stopped right in front of her, she had an inclination to turn and run from the room.

"Maybe this isn't such a good idea," she managed to say.

He put his fingers under her chin and coaxed her to lift her head higher. She met the softness of his eyes. That open window she was starting to think very few people ever saw.

"Don't be afraid," he said. "I won't hurt you."

And she melted. The sound of his raspy voice trickled through her nerves. Real trust stole over her.

He touched his lips to hers. Gentle. Soft. His eyes were still open, watching her, assessing, gauging. He lifted one of her hands and put it on his chest. She flattened her palm there, feeling a rekindled spark ignite. She put her other hand next to it. His skin was smooth and lightly haired.

Leaning closer, she bent her head and pressed her mouth on his chest between her hands, breathing him in, kissing her way up his neck, along his jaw, until she found his mouth again.

He slid his hands around her waist, drawing her with him away from the door. Turning her, he backed her up until he had her closer to the bed.

Taking the hem of her dress in his hands, he pulled it up her body, moving slow, as though knowing anything too fast would spook her into withdrawing. He couldn't know how right he was. Her heart pounded from more than desire as he lifted the dress over her head and dropped it to the side of the bed. She hadn't worn a bra, so the only things left were her underwear and sandals.

Wrapping his arm around her, he knelt on the bed, lowering her gently to the mattress. Sliding her up the bed so that they both fit on it, he kissed her. Soft, quick touches. Sometimes lingering. She drifted into a fine eddy, let herself get lost in the feelings that came with it.

He moved down her neck, leaving a trail of fireworks along the way. His hands roamed down her waist and over her hips to her thighs. He reached her breasts and bestowed each with tender kisses, taking one of her nipples into his mouth and circling it with his tongue.

Haley bracketed his head with her hands, wanting that mouth back on hers. He obliged her, kissing her harder now. Kissing her endlessly. Until finally he seemed to have to break away. Breathless, he rose up onto his knees, straddling one of her legs as he reached for the button of his jeans. He looked his fill of her lying on the bed, those light blue eyes taking in every inch of her body. Instead of frightening her, it intrigued her and heated her blood.

The zipper went down and he pushed the jeans over his hips. His underwear went down, too. Working his way out of the rest of his clothes, he positioned himself between her legs, watching her again.

He stopped, kneeling over her. Hesitant. Mindful of her needs. Her fears. Intrigue won over fear. Intrigue. And trust. The impact of that bathed her senses. Trust. Did she trust him?

Yes. On the most intimate level.

Rolling onto her hip, she let him know what she wanted. He lay on his back, a soft grin pushing up his mouth as she climbed on top of him. He put his hands on her hips and glided them around to her back as she leaned forward. Her hair fell like a curtain beside their faces. She kissed his grinning mouth. She moved on to his throat and reached his chest, hearing and seeing his excited breathing. His stomach muscles tightened as she kissed her way down his body. He put his hands on her shoulders, curving over the joints. Ready to stop her if it got too torturous.

She ran her tongue over his warm flesh, loving the texture and the way he responded. He wanted her. She marveled over that, over the way he made her yearn to give him as much pleasure as he would give her. She wanted him to know this act of love would not be forgotten. Not by her.

Kissing her way back up his torso, she toyed with his chest, all the while gliding her hands over him, his sides, his arms.

Then she lowered her body onto his. Their nakedness generated warmth and the intimate contact made her press her hips more firmly to his, moving over his erection, the only barrier her underwear.

He swore in French again, this time sounding rough and unsteady. The idea of Rem unsteady gave her a triumphant sense of gladness. That she could render him that way with only her mouth. A man like Rem…

She touched her mouth to his for a sweet kiss, but he'd taken all he could of her attention. With a smooth roll, he had her underneath him again.

He kissed her long and deep while his hand ran over her breast and down her side. He hooked her underwear with his fingers and slid them down. She kicked them free of her legs, but she still had on her sandals.

Rem must have known it all along, because now he moved down one of her legs, brushing kisses along her inner thigh as though he'd planned it all along. Down her knee. Her lower leg. She barely noticed when he peeled off her sandals. They landed one after the other with soft thuds on the floor.

Now he crawled back up toward her, between her legs, spreading them wider as he moved. At the juncture of her thighs, he stopped, looking up at her with dark desire humming in his eyes. The first touch of his tongue made her put her head back onto the bed and shut her eyes. He was excruciatingly gentle, each brush sending shards of sensation spinning outward from where he touched. He slid his stubbly chin against her softness. The sensations intensified. A sound erupted from her, one she had no control over.

He didn't stop. He kept strumming her nerve endings, always, always…relentlessly gentle. Just when she thought she was going to explode, he withdrew.

"Don't stop," she breathed, only then aware of how audible her breathing was.

Taking her mouth into a long, wet kiss, he maneuvered the tip of his erection where his mouth had been.

The invasion made her stiffen. He kissed her cheek and then the skin near her ear.

"It's me doing this to you," he told her, pushing himself a little deeper. "It's me."

Rem. It was Rem filling her. No one else. She gripped his arms, digging her fingers into his hard-muscled skin.

He lifted his head to look at her. "Haley."

She wondered if she looked as vulnerable as she felt.

He pulled back and pushed in again, going deeper than before. Pressure stretched her inner walls. He pushed in more. More. Until he lodged himself all the way in.

Haley broke into a cold sweat. But instead of enduring him pounding her, she ended up waiting. He didn't move. He went still inside her, letting her grow accustomed to him.

She began to relax. Her legs trembled again as tension eased from her muscles. She began to see the way he was looking at her. Really see it. Intent on giving her pleasure. Intent on obliterating Iraq from her mind.

"Rem," she whispered.

With a satisfied groan, he moved. Each thrust touched off incredible feelings that radiated and burst. He moved faster. Sensation intensified. She came hard on him, squeezing his rigid flesh, pulling another groan from him.

He did pound her then, but it wasn't long before he reached his own release. As he lay on her, she knew she'd never felt more alive in her life. Complete. Healed. Herself again.

She sighed, long and content. *Welcome back*.

Chapter 10

Haley woke with a long stretch and a moan. She blinked her eyes open, feeling a delicious fatigue. Sunlight poured through the window. The room was quiet.

She rolled onto her back and looked beside her. Rem was gone. She put her hand on the sheets where he'd been. No longer warm from his body heat.

She sat upright. The blankets fell away and cool air brushed bare skin. He was nowhere in the room. She heard no sounds from the bathroom, either. Where was he? A stab of disappointment gripped her. Couldn't he have waited for her to wake up? Why had he sneaked away like this? Again.

She knew, of course. He'd gone to the second *hawaladar*.

Pulling the covers aside, she rose from the bed. She dressed in jeans and a white short-sleeved T-shirt, wondering what she should do. Wait for him? She'd all but gone crazy the last time she'd tried that. Maybe she'd go down for some coffee and breakfast. If anything it would kill some time. She found her wallet in Rem's duffel bag and paused in the bathroom to put her hair up before leaving the room.

On the main level, she headed for the brasserie. Growing aware of a presence behind her, she glanced over her shoulder.

A man walked a few paces back, a cell phone to his ear. He saw her and looked away. But something in the way he spoke into the phone alerted her. Too quiet. Too discreet.

Heart springing into faster beats, she faced forward and walked faster. Should she try to go back to the room? She'd have to turn around to do that, and then she'd have to get past the man. Maybe she was overreacting.

She searched the lobby. It was nearly empty of people this morning. She spotted the front entrance. There were two cabs parked in front. She headed there.

Outside, she looked behind her. The man had put away his cell and was still following her. Again, he looked away when he caught her glance.

"Crap," Haley hissed lowly. She opened the door to one of the cabs and climbed in.

"Wenceslas Square," she told the cab driver.

The dark-haired, dark-skinned man pulled into traffic. Haley twisted to look behind the car. Sure enough, the man had gotten into the second cab.

She faced forward. "Drive faster."

The driver looked in his rearview mirror and didn't respond. Nor did he drive faster. Traffic was heavy.

"Stop the car!" she yelled.

He pulled to the side of the road and after tossing money at his lap, she bolted.

Wenceslas Square and the shop where Rem had gone to find the *hawaladar* wasn't far from here. Besides, she didn't want to lead the man following her to Rem. And she needed Rem right now.

She ran. A quick check confirmed the other cab had stopped, too. She ran into a café. Dodged tables and gaping people on her way back to the kitchen. A man shouted at her in a foreign language. She spotted a back door and ran for it. Outside, she ran up an alley until she came to another door. She tried it. Locked. She ran to another one. This one was open. She ran inside of a tea and coffee shop, making her way from the back room to the front, where people took up two small, round tables and a waitress looked over her shoulder at Haley as she ran past. Back outside, she ran up the street toward the boutique where Rem had gone.

At last, she saw a sign above a shop window that said Josef's. Breathing hard, she looked down the street. No one followed. She opened the door and stepped inside. It was quiet. No one else was in the shop, not even a clerk. What if Rem was no longer here?

She saw a door leading to a back room and went there. Opening it, she peered into what appeared to be a stockroom and office all in one. She entered, leaving the door open behind her. Movement to her left made her jump. Rem put his gun back into the waist of his jeans.

"Rem." She breathed her relief and more. Seeing him after what had transpired between them felt different now. More intimate. Which also made her feel vulnerable.

"What the hell are you doing here?" he asked.

That settled her well enough. She focused on the present. "Someone followed me. I lost them before I came here, but he was in the lobby at the hotel. I was going to grab breakfast when I noticed him."

He went to the door, opening it to check the front of the shop. When he closed it, she knew no one had come in after her.

She spotted a computer on a small desk. It was on and the email software was open. Rem had been searching it. Something on the floor caught her attention. Two feet stuck out from behind a stack of boxes. A man was lying there.

She shot Rem a glance. His jaw flexed and his eyes turned hard with angst.

"What did you do?" She didn't wait for him to answer. She

marched toward the man on the floor. Rem put his arm out and stopped her like a gate. She pushed his arm and forced her way past him. She rounded the stack of boxes and sucked in a shocked breath of air.

A man lay in a pool of blood, some of it having soaked into the floor-level boxes. He'd been shot in the chest.

The second *hawaladar*.

She gagged and put her hand over her mouth. When the nausea faded, she faced Rem. "What happened?"

With intensifying annoyance, he turned back to the computer and didn't answer.

She looked at the body again, at the signs of struggle around the room. Tipped over boxes. Paper. Blood...

Rem continued to click away at the computer.

"Why did you kill him?" She was too appalled not to stop and think. After sleeping with him...

He clicked the computer mouse, opening an e-mail. "What makes you think I'm the one who killed him?"

"Didn't you?" Confused emotion whirled inside her. It looked as if he had, but...

He straightened from the computer and sent her a furious glance.

A sound in the front of the shop made them both look toward the door. Rem pulled out his gun.

"Stay here," he ordered with a feral gaze arrowed at her, and went through the door.

Haley followed, but kept herself concealed at the door. She heard talking, harsh at first, then calmer. Rem reappeared, gun once again stowed in the waist of his jeans and another man following.

She moved aside when Rem and the man entered. The man had dark hair and was not very tall. His dark eyes found the man on the floor and with a sound of anguish, went there.

"He said he was a friend of Josef's," Rem told her. "His name is Alan."

After a moment, Alan straightened from the body and came around the boxes, wiping his eyes as he stopped before Rem and Haley.

"You found him this way?" Alan asked Rem.

When Rem nodded, Haley struggled whether to believe it was the truth. Alan clearly was Josef's friend. If Rem had killed Josef, wouldn't he want to appear innocent? And yet...

"You are that man," Alan said. "The one who is looking for Farid. You are Rem D'Evereux. No?"

Haley's awareness sharpened and she sensed Rem do the same.

"How do you know me?"

"Josef told me about you. He said that Ammar warned him you might come. Josef told me he was afraid of what Ammar would do. He also said that if anything were to happen to him, I was to find you. Come." Alan headed for the door. "I have something to give you."

Haley exchanged a glance with Rem, just as surprised as him. They followed the short man out of the shop. Haley searched with Rem for the man who'd followed her. He looked at her and she shook her head. She didn't see him. Alan led them into the shop next to Josef's. A gift shop filled with colorful and gaudy baubles. Behind the counter, Alan bent and retrieved a manila envelope.

Rem opened it and slipped out a handwritten note with a South American address. Argentina. Locke had told him the truth.

"Josef said if you came and he was dead, that he hopes this information will help you avenge him. He hoped you would kill Farid and his son."

"Are you sure Farid went back to his ranch in Argentina?" Rem asked. "It's the first place our government would look."

Haley could see Rem's disbelief, and maybe his chagrin that he hadn't thought of it himself before now.

"Josef said that Farid was a fool for hiding in plain sight. He said if your government didn't find him, that he hoped you would. He was counting on it. If you would have come before Ammar got here, he would have told you everything himself."

"Wouldn't that be dangerous for him?" Haley said.

"The only danger Josef faced was from Farid and his son. Josef was an honest man. Farid and his son are not."

"I'll find Farid," Rem said.

Alan nodded, the satisfaction of vengeance in his eyes. "Then on behalf of Josef, I thank you."

Rem led Haley out of the shop. He ought to be celebrating finally locating Farid, after all the careful planning and patience. Instead, all he felt was anger. It consumed him. He still couldn't believe Haley actually thought he'd killed Josef. How easy it had been for her to think it, as if it were the most natural thing in the world for him to kill a man for not telling him what he wanted to know. Whatever happened to her observation that he wouldn't have killed the courier without a good and just reason?

Rem caught himself. What the hell was he doing? Why did her opinion of him matter so much?

It didn't help that thoughts of last night kept filtering into his head. Watching the haunting effects of Iraq fade in the wake of Haley's passion. The sight of her face would be forever burned into his memory. He doubted if any other challenge had ever felt more gratifying. Wiping a terrible experience from a beautiful woman's mind, an experience that didn't belong in such a pure and lovely body. He'd exulted that he'd been the man to do that for her, if only for a few incredible moments.

He'd tasted that. Intoxicating pleasure. Nothing standing in the way of its absolute intensity.

Now she was contradicting herself, believing he'd murdered an innocent man for not giving him what he wanted. Had she been playing him all this time? Why? To uncover what he was hiding? Maybe Cullen had put her up to the task. Maybe he'd learned more than he'd let on and Haley was his way to get Rem, put another notch on his long list of conquests.

Waving down a cab, he opened the back door for Haley, looking up and down the street before getting in after her. He spotted a dark car parked along the street with three men inside. Ammar. Whoever had tailed Haley had probably summoned him. He smiled. Now Ammar would follow him to South America, and after Rem killed him, he'd take care of Farid.

"Rem."

He turned his head to see Haley nodding toward the black car. He faced forward. "I know."

"We don't want them to know we're going to South America," she said. "How are we going to lose them?"

He didn't answer, just waved a cab and opened the back door for her. She hesitated before getting in, sending him a purposeful look, one full of disbelief.

"It's Ammar," she said.

"I know. Get in."

"If we don't lose them, they'll know where we're going. They'll follow us."

"Get in the cab."

She stared at him. But finally she complied, sliding over on the backseat with sharp blue eyes focused on him intently.

"Are you mad about earlier?" she asked.

Knowing she was referring to her quick assumption that he'd killed Josef, he leaned back against the seat and let her assumption take flight.

"I'm sorry I…" Her pause revealed her struggle to find words. "It's just…I didn't know what happened."

"It's what anyone would have thought at first." But he hated how it got to him, even for a few seconds, that she'd thought he'd mercilessly killed someone. He was not accustomed to caring what people thought of him. That she made him care threw him into a tailspin. He didn't know what to do with all the clashing emotions. He was a merc. He was a merc who'd killed many, many times. But he was a merc who'd never taken innocent lives. Most people who knew anything about him shied away. The ones who didn't were just like him. They understood what he did. But Haley…she twisted that concept of merc-with-a-purpose around in his heart until he could find no beginning or end in his soul.

Damn it! He was who he was. Why couldn't she accept that?

"Rem—"

"Just let it go, Haley. It's done. Over."

Her sea-blue eyes beckoned him. "I know you wouldn't have done it without a good reason."

"You'll change your mind after South America."

That made her pause again, only this time in contemplative thought. She glanced out the back window. Rem didn't have to look with her to know Ammar and his men followed. But what had she ascertained in that brilliant mind of hers? He was beginning to think the step ahead he'd thought he'd maintained was shortening faster than he was ready.

"What are you going to do there?" she asked, confirming his worry.

The cab came to a stop in front of the Prague Marriott Hotel. Without answering, he paid the fare and asked the driver to wait for them.

He opened the cab door and would have gotten out, but Haley's hand on his arm stopped him. He looked over at her.

"No matter what you intend to do," she said, her magnificent eyes intent, and then her smooth, sultry voice going in for the kill, "I trust you."

The declaration arrowed through him. It found his weakness. The one Ammar knew too well. The one Rem tried so hard to avoid. And here she was, doing things to him that could ruin all his plans. His well-thought-out revenge. He needed that revenge. When he got it, he just might be able to go on with his life, to find the peace that he'd been seeking for so many years.

But that peace came without compromise. He wasn't changing for anyone, least of all Haley. She represented too much of what had been denied him through his hardest times.

"You shouldn't," he said with more meaning coming out in his tone than made him comfortable.

And of course, she was relentless.

"I wasn't talking about my heart."

No, she was talking about killing with a reason. He battled with defenses that bordered on resentment, knowing his ego was fighting for the limelight. "Cullen was right about one thing, Haley. This *is* personal for me."

She was totally unflustered. "I know," she said tartly. "I also know you're hiding something from me. Or maybe it's Cullen you fear. But whatever it is, I'm going to find out, and when I do, I promise I won't think less of you."

He looked into her beautiful eyes, lingering in the gaze they shared. Bittersweet realization struck him that she would, in fact, uncover his secret. And when she did, the two of them could never be.

"Be careful what you promise, sweetheart," he said, the gruffness in his voice manifested by his emotion. "Some promises are impossible to keep."

Chapter 11

Rem's words kept running through her head. Haley hadn't said much on their way to Foz do Iguacu, which the locals called Foz. She was too preoccupied with her thoughts. Now she sat across from him at an outdoor table of a not-so-nice bar on the main drag, enduring his occasional and assessing glances between his surveillance of the street.

Why was he so sure she'd think less of him when she discovered what he was hiding? Had he done something to earn it? Another wayward set of circumstances not unlike the one when he was fourteen that had made him turn to drugs to survive? Or was he as unabashedly disreputable as he let people believe?

That last thought disconcerted her. How could she be so wrong about the only man who'd been able to breach the walls she'd erected after Iraq? Or had it required a man like him and she just hadn't realized that yet? Maybe exactly what she'd needed was a ruthless man with good intentions in bed. Ruthless men had violated her in Iraq, despite her lack of memory of the attack. It made perfect sense that someone equally frightening would erase the negativity of her ordeal by treating her gently in the most intimate situation.

The idea of bringing terrorists down appealed to her, and on a deeper level she could relate to Rem's thirst for blood. But he was so scary about it. Quiet. Lurking. Certain of his ability. She'd sensed that about him the first second she'd seen him outside Habib's market.

Music thumped from inside the bar. People walked by in front of the patio, talking, laughing, speaking Portuguese or Spanish. Though the sun had set long ago, the heavy heat made her feel sticky. Rem shifted in his chair, the hem of his short-sleeved shirt molding for a second over the shape of the pistol tucked in the waist of his jeans. He'd bought it and another one from a man they'd met earlier that day, since they couldn't fly armed. It had bothered her that he'd known the man and made her wonder when he'd contacted him. She didn't like his secrets.

She was in a potentially volatile area of Brazil with a dangerous man whose agenda involved more than getting the men who'd tortured and killed his sister. Why did he want Ammar to follow them? Because she knew that was his intention back in Prague. Was that why he stole the diamonds? He had to know Ammar would do anything to get them back. If Rem took them to South America, where he'd find Farid, Ammar was sure to trail them. Did he want them both in the same place to make it easier to move in for the kill?

Why keep it from her, then? Did he have some other connection with Ammar and Farid? Maybe it was his relationship with the two that he meant to keep buried. A chill cruised over her sweat-dampened skin. No. Anything but that. He couldn't have a history with terrorists. He just couldn't.

"What will you do if Ammar doesn't follow you?" she asked. No getting around what she insinuated. She knew he'd intended exactly that—for Ammar to follow the diamonds.

His eyes moved from perusing the street to her. "He'll come."

At least he didn't deny it. "Is that why you took the diamonds?"

He resumed his study of the street, calm as could be. It was unnerving how unruffled he was.

"What will you do with them when it's over?"

"I don't know," he said without looking at her.

"Are you going to sell them and keep the money?"

She watched his brow lower as her meaning sank in. His attention returned to her. "What am I supposed to do with them?" He snorted. "Or maybe the more appropriate question is, what would Cullen do with them?"

"I don't understand your obsession with Cullen." Even though she did. "It doesn't matter what he'd do with the diamonds. What are *you* going to do with them?"

"Sell them to someone I know and buy a really nice yacht."

"Your sarcasm tells me all I need to know." She tossed her hair away from her face and looked away.

"You want to believe I'll be like everyone else and do the *noble* thing, is that it? Like give it to a popular charity?"

"No, I would never expect you to do anything so ordinary."

"I never pretended to be anything but who I am."

"Nope, you never did."

She didn't have to see him to know he sat over there stewing. "The money from those diamonds would allow me to gear my company with state-of-the-art equipment," he said at last.

But she heard the cynicism in his tone. "Oh, you mean your *rogue* private military company?" She couldn't stop the emotion from flying along with the words. "Is that the one we're talking about?"

"The one I took over from Dane after he was so conveniently killed? Yes, that would be the one."

"Right. *Pioneer* Security *Consultants*. And you say you aren't pretending?"

"To be like Cullen? No. I never pretend to be what I am not."

"Then why the noble name, hmm?"

He stood from the chair and took a menacing step over to her. Leaning down, he took both her arms in his grasp and pulled her to her feet. She lost her breath as the full impact of his angry face loomed above her. So much intensity. The strength of his personality engulfed her. Drive. Purpose. Conviction. He had it all in glorious abundance. It fascinated her how he could miss seeing it himself.

"Because, while I'm not like the great and mighty Cullen McQueen, neither am I like *Dane Charter*."

He practically spat the last name.

Didn't he realize all he'd done was prove her point? It didn't matter, though. He believed he didn't belong in the same circles as men like Cullen, and that spelled out only one thing to her. When they returned to the States, he wouldn't want any more to do with her. She traveled among people like Cullen. He'd leave her to find someone he thought was more like him.

Haley stepped back, shrugging her shoulders and arms to loosen his hold on her. He let her go.

She wasn't sure how she felt about that revelation. Did she want to continue this when they arrived back home? She couldn't stop herself from taking in his body, big and hard and sexy. She met his eyes, watching her with all that intensity. God, she loved that about him. Too much. If she wasn't careful, she'd fall too much for him and have to deal with losing him later.

Turning, she left the sidewalk restaurant to find a cab. It was a short drive to their hotel from here. The Tropical das Cataratas hotel was a sprawling colonial-style building in the

Iguacu National Park, surrounded by dense jungle. Their room had a stunning partial view of the Iguacu Falls.

A figure leaning against the wall of the building across the street pulled her attention away from her thoughts. Rem must have seen him, too. He tugged her to a stop, turning her into his arms. She came against his body and felt him slide his arms around her, his hands on her back.

She marveled at the look of hungry desire on his face. Was he only acting?

"Let's order room service when we get back to the hotel," he said.

Was this for the benefit of the stranger? "What are you doing, Rem?"

"We haven't eaten yet."

"Sure. Room service." She wasn't in the mood to play along with him. Not after wondering if he had a closer connection to Ammar than he'd allowed anyone to know so far.

He leaned closer.

"Don't you dare," she warned.

"I'm going to kiss you. Make it look good."

"Rem, don't."

His lips pressed against hers. She stared up at him, his eyes still open, too. He lifted his head and a crooked grin gave him the look of a wily pirate.

She couldn't help her adoration. "Why are you doing this?" The fire had left her voice. It had moved to her heart.

"One," he kissed her softly, melting her further. "I want to." He kissed her again. "And two, it will make it look like I'm distracted."

His mouth moved over hers, sending delicious sensation flying through her nerve endings.

"You mean you're not?" she whispered against his lips.

He smiled sexily and chuckled. "No." He kissed her harder. "I am."

The sound of his chuckle was a rarity, a gift. It incited her desire.

Angling her head, she opened her mouth and slid her arms over his muscular shoulders, letting the feel of his strength and warmth fuel her further. His hands pulled her tighter against him.

She found his tongue and toyed with it, until the toying changed to an intimate dance. His breaths blew faster onto her skin. She pressed her breasts firmer against his hard chest. With a low grunt, his hands slid to her rear and he pressed her against his growing hardness.

"Let's go to the room," he rasped. He didn't sound like he was acting.

"Rem." Hearing the loss of control in her own voice, she knew going to the room would be a huge mistake just now.

"I want you."

She believed him.

He broke apart from the kiss and took hold of her hand, lacing his fingers with hers. She forgot to look for the stranger before Rem flagged down a cab. His hands caressed her as he guided her inside, slid off her as she sat in the backseat. He sat close, telling the driver where to take them before leaning toward her, caging her with his bulk.

He didn't look through the back window. He just kissed her.

She put her hand on his chest, meaning to stop him, but the feel of his mouth on hers was too strong to turn away. He kissed her all the way back to the hotel. There, he fumbled with money to pay the driver, and then took her hand and hurried toward the elevator.

Heat throbbed between her legs as the elevator door closed behind them and another couple. Her heart beat fast and she had to conceal her breathing. When the doors slid open on their floor, he pulled her behind him, walking with long strides toward their room. He wasn't pretending anymore, and she was a fool for wanting him this way.

Inside the room, she moved away from him, folding her arms and going over to the only window. She had to think about this. Too much more of him would have her falling madly in love. Not trusting him to be there for her when this was over, that seemed pretty stupid to her right now.

She heard him approach from behind. Heard his breathing. Felt his heat. He put his hands on the curve of her shoulders and pressed a kiss on her back. Then her neck. Haley tilted her head and closed her eyes, unable to resist the sensation.

"Rem—"

"Shhh."

"I…" His mouth did incredible things to her jaw. The corner of her mouth. His hands slid over her lower stomach, causing the muscles there to spasm in pleasured response.

"I don't want to do this," she breathed, opening her eyes.

"It'll be even better than the last time," he said, kissing his way back down her neck.

His hands moved up to cover her breasts. She moaned and closed her eyes again. That was what she was afraid of. That it would be better. Better than anything she'd felt in her life.

"Rem…please. Stop."

His hands went back to her stomach and went still. He lifted his mouth off her neck. "What's the matter?"

She didn't know how to tell him. Should she come right out and ask him what he was hiding? Would he tell her?

He straightened and moved back a step. She turned to face him. And saw the passion still in his eyes, and the restraint to respect her wishes.

"Tell me," he said.

She hesitated. "What aren't you telling me about Ammar?"

It took him a few seconds to answer. "What makes you think there's something I know about Ammar?"

She could see he was hedging. "Why can't you tell me?"

"He killed my sister."

"What else did he do?"

"Isn't that enough?"

"That's not what I mean." She sighed and lifted her hands in exasperation. "I just…I…I have this feeling there's more between you and Ammar than you've let on."

Seeing every trace of affection leave his eyes, Haley tensed. A mask of defensiveness hardened his features. Was this why he always argued with her about the goodness she saw in him?

"Oh, my God. There is."

"Not the way you're thinking."

"How long have you known him?"

His mouth tightened and his jaw muscles flexed.

Something Cullen had said came to her. "The drug deal. Dane Charter was moving drugs for Ammar. Did you have anything to do with that? Did you find out about it and interfere?" Her mind whirled with speeding thoughts. "Is that the reason Dane was killed?"

Anger made its way past the indifferent mask.

Why did that make him angry? The fact he was convinced her she was on to something. "What happened?"

"It doesn't matter."

"You don't think? Isn't that the real reason your sister was killed?"

"Stop."

"What did you do?"

He just stood there looking at her with tumultuous emotion building in his expression.

"Why did Ammar come after your sister?" She refused to back down.

"I killed Farid's cousin."

"What about the drugs?"

Still, he didn't give an inch.

"Just tell me what happened, Rem."

"I stopped a deal from happening."

"Ammar's?"

"Dane's."

"But they came from Ammar, right?"

"Yes."

Something didn't add up. Why would Ammar come after Rem and his sister if he'd already sold the drugs to Dane?

Unless Rem took them before Dane could get them from Ammar. But why would he do that?

"Did you make it look like Dane was the one who stole the drugs?" she asked, thinking out loud.

She didn't expect Rem to help her much, and he didn't.

"How did Ammar discover it was you?" A chill of horror streamed through her. "Your sister." Ammar and his men had tortured her, and likely raped her after she told them everything she knew. The agony gripping Rem's face confirmed it. Haley put her hand over her mouth but couldn't muffle the sound of anguish that came from her.

Was that the reason he didn't tell her and Cullen everything? Because he couldn't? The guilt must have all but destroyed him. She moved toward him, and when she was close enough, reached up to take his face between her hands.

"I'm so sorry."

Instead of softening emotion—what she expected to see— she saw hardened withdrawal. He curled his hands around her wrists and lowered her hands, stepping back as he released her.

The shock of coldness spread inside her. There was more. More that he wasn't telling her. His sister talking after being tortured wasn't the reason. Not the only one. And it crushed her to know he might be hiding something. Darker than anything else she already knew about him. Why else couldn't he talk about it?

A clicking sound woke Haley. She blinked her eyes open and looked to her right. Rem lay beside her, his arm over her waist. That hand slid off her and moved under the pillow below his head. She caught the glint of metal in the dim light coming thought the window. They'd left the curtains open.

The floor creaked from across the dark room. Haley looked there but couldn't see anything. Was someone in the hall outside their door? A fraction of a second later, Rem shoved her off the bed. She landed with a grunt and a thud onto the wood floor, taking covers with her. She heard the distinctive sound of silenced gunshots and scrambled to untangle herself from the blanket and sheet. The mattress jounced as Rem jumped off the bed.

Haley kicked the last of the blankets free and rolled onto her hands and knees. Careful to keep the bed between her and any bullets the intruder might fire her way, she peered through the shadows above the mattress.

Two figures wrestled, rolling until one straddled the other. Rem. She recognized his form. He slammed the intruder's hand against the hard wood floor until the gun clattered free from his grasp. Shoving the gun so it slid out of reach, he hit the man with his pistol. The man blocked Rem's second attempt to hit him with the weapon. The gun was knocked loose and fell to the floor. Rem deflected the man's swinging fist and punched him.

Haley climbed to her feet and moved to the lamp beside the bed. She clicked on the light. An Arab-looking man with a thick black beard and cold brown eyes wrestled his way out from under Rem. He staggered as Rem advanced toward him. Grabbing the black-bearded man's brown T-shirt, Rem slammed his fist into the man's face. Again and again. The man stumbled backward, falling with his back against the glass door. He turned and slid the door open, stumbling outside onto the balcony. He gripped the stone rail and faced Rem. Pushing off the rail, he charged for Rem. But Rem was ready and deflected the Arab man's attempt to hit him. He chopped the back of the man's head with his hand. Rem caught him as he went limp and lifted. Swinging the body over the rail, he let the man's body fall.

Haley covered her mouth with a startled gasp. She hadn't expected Rem to do something so drastic. She hurried outside, bracing her hands on the rail beside Rem. They were on the third level, and the man's body was sprawled on the artfully landscaped ground in broken angles. Was he dead?

Something dark and unwanted curled through her. She couldn't stop staring at the body. Lifeless. Broken. Flashes of memory assaulted her.

Images of her Iraqi captors hitting her invaded her failing defenses. Slapping her face. Driving the butts of their rifles against her ribs. Slamming the hard metal against her shins. One of them bringing his face close to hers, growling obscenities, telling her what he was going to do to her body in badly broken English.

She heard her own whimper. No. No. She didn't want to remember any more. What if she hadn't gone unconscious before they started doing what the doctors had confirmed they'd done?

Her hand trembled over her mouth. Tears burned her eyes.

Ripping clothes. More punching...

"Haley?" Rem put his bloody hand on her shoulder.

She flinched and backed away, looking at him but only seeing the faces of her captors abusing her. More tearing clothes. Another hard blow to her head. It was more than she'd ever remembered.

"No," she whispered, her whole body quivering. She put her hands to her ears, not wanting to hear her own screams piercing her mind.

"Are you hurt?" Rem advanced toward her. She backed into the room. "Were you hit?" His eyes frantically searched for wounds.

She stared at his hand, only a minor scrape there, but it was enough to keep the haunting memories alive. He looked at his hand as if he'd noticed her fixation. She moved back until she felt the bed and sat down on the mattress, wishing she could push the horror out of her mind.

Rem came to her, kneeling on one knee and gripping her arms. Careful not to look at the blood, she met eyes that were full of intense concern. She didn't want it. She didn't want the memories to keep running through her head. Better to put them aside, to not let them linger any longer. Bury them, as always. Bury them like they were dead.

"Are you all right?" he asked.

Shakily, she nodded, digging her fingers through her hair and lowering her hands to her lap.

"What happened to you just now?"

She shook her head. She had to stop him from talking about it.

"Did you remember something?"

How did he guess it? She averted her eyes, wishing he hadn't. "Don't."

"You remember?"

She shook her head again. "Don't, Rem."

"Haley, you should talk about it. Maybe it'll help."

Now she turned to look at him. "No. It won't help."

He breathed out a heavy sigh but didn't push her. "I wish there was something I could do."

She reached up and put her hand on his cheek. "You can't bully it out of my head."

He covered her hand with his uninjured one and turned his head until his lips pressed against her palm. His kisses felt warm and soft, and tingles strummed in her skin. Too soon, he took her hands in his and lowered them to her lap. Then his eyes found hers and the intensity of them made her breath catch.

"If you ever do remember, I hope I'm with you," he said. "I may not be able to fight them for you, but I can hold you until it passes."

Such sweet sentiments from such a brawny man seemed at odds, and yet…not. She smiled with the thought.

He smiled back, more of a crooked grin. "How did you ever get Cullen to hire you? Didn't he think your history would pose a problem? I would have."

"I knew his secretary. Odelia Frank. I went to see her after I recovered. She told Cullen about me and he invited me to Roaring Creek for a…a kind of interview."

Rem's grin expanded a little. "You mean he interrogated you?"

She knew he meant the same way Cullen had interrogated him. "He made sure I was emotionally sound."

"Were you?"

"Yes," she answered, a bit too quickly.

"It must have helped that you didn't remember anything about what happened."

She was relieved he didn't press her on her emotional state after returning from the hospital. She'd been so raw on the inside, but she had fooled everyone by hiding just how deep the pain had gone.

"Yes," she said in a calmer tone.

"What if you do remember?"

"I won't."

"But what if you do? Someday you probably will. Someday you might be ready."

The thought of remembering the awfulness of what happened to her was a horror too great to explore. "Uh-uh." She shook her head. "No."

"Don't you see? What you're doing, everything you've done since Iraq, has led to this. You're doing this to fight back, but what it's leading to is remembering. And I think you need to remember before you can put it all behind you."

"It's not about whether I remember or not. It's better if I don't remember. I don't want to carry that ugliness with me the rest of my life. This is about fighting injustice. I'm fighting men who do terrible things to innocent people."

"A noble cause, I won't argue with you there, but that cause is going to force you to face what you most want to keep buried."

She stared into his blue eyes. Was she doing that? And how ironic was it that Rem was the man who triggered it. She caught herself.

"I don't want to remember." Haley hoped that day would never come. Because if it did, she was pretty sure it would destroy her.

Chapter 12

Haley glanced at Rem from the passenger seat of the Jeep he'd rented. They bounced and jerked along the shoddy dirt road, the jungle a tangled mess around them. After the way Rem had disposed of the attacker's body, it was time for them to leave. But taking her to a remote location seemed to go against Rem's usual tendency to stay in public, in plain sight for Ammar to see.

"Where are we going?" she asked.

"There's a place not far from here."

"Why so isolated? Are you having second thoughts?"

He glanced at her but didn't answer. The way he adjusted his grip on the wheel and ran his fingers through his hair told her he struggled with whatever decision he'd made, whatever had made him bring her here, deep in the jungle, away from everyone, including Ammar.

A few minutes later, he stopped the Jeep at a small shack. Haley got out and followed him inside. A small sitting area and adjacent kitchen made up the main room, and two doors led to a bathroom and a bedroom. It was dusty but not disgusting, as she'd been expecting.

"How did you find this place?" she asked.

"I know the man who owns it."

She nodded. He probably knew a lot of people who helped him along his way.

"What are we going to do?"

He dropped a duffel bag on the bed and unzipped it.

"Why didn't we come here when we first arrived?" she pressed. "Why the stop at the hotel?"

He took out the satellite phone and put it on the mattress. "I had to make sure Ammar followed. Until I knew he was here."

"And when he discovers you killed the man he sent after us?"

"He'll be looking for me."

"And, of course, you want that."

"I don't want him to find us here."

She raised her brow.

"You'll be safe here while I go back into town to find him," he answered her silent question.

"You want me to wait here."

"Haley—"

"No." She moved across the small room to stand in front of him by the bed. "I'm not going to let you take on Ammar all by yourself. I can help you."

"You're staying here."

She folded her arms and let her eyes tell him what she thought. She didn't have to obey him.

"You'll only get in the way," he said.

"I will not." She unfolded her arms and put one hand on her hip. "You know I'm capable, Rem."

"You're not coming with me," he said, his tone delivering more force.

"You of all people should know better than to treat me like a victim."

"This is going to be dangerous."

"All the more reason for me to go with you."

She saw his refusal to bend and gave up arguing. Instead, she decided to change her tactic. "Rem, why are you doing this? Surely you know Farid will have more men than you can fight all by yourself."

"And you'll make that much of a difference?"

"We could call Cullen."

A cynical grunt came from him.

"He can send backup."

The sound of a car pulling to a stop outside had Haley turning with Rem. He glanced at her once before moving to his gun. Haley found the other one and went to a window, standing off to the side to peer outside. Two men got out of a black SUV.

Shock fired through Haley. "How did he find us?"

"I'd like to know that, too. We weren't followed."

She looked at him and he met her gaze, both of them sharing questions neither had to voice.

"The man who owns this place?" she said. "Does Ammar know he's your friend?"

"I didn't think so, but he worked on Farid's ranch. I met him when I was on assignment there."

"Ammar must have figured it out."

Rem nodded. "Or someone else did and told him."

Haley faced the window again. Holding automatic weapons, two of the men stood near the SUV, scanning the area. Ammar climbed out of the vehicle.

Rem put the satellite phone into the duffel bag. "Come on." He took her hand and led her to a back door. Outside, she followed him along the side of the building.

When he stopped at the corner, she peered around his big arm while he adjusted the duffel over his shoulder and adjusted his grip on his gun. Ammar and one of the men had reached the front door. The third walked to the opposite side of the building, disappearing around the corner. The man still with Ammar kicked the front door in and entered. Ammar followed.

Rem tugged her into a run toward the Jeep. She slammed the passenger door just as Rem started the engine and put it into gear.

Bullets pinged and clanged as Rem drove away. Haley twisted on the seat to see Ammar and the other two men running toward the SUV. Rem sped down the long, bumpy dirt road. Swerving onto the main road, he righted the Jeep. But the SUV was gaining on them.

Haley glanced at Rem. His eyes turned from the rearview mirror to her.

The SUV rammed them from behind. Rem almost lost control. When the SUV drew alongside them and rammed the side, he did. The Jeep rolled. Haley lost her gun as she was thrown from the vehicle. She landed on the soggy edge of a swamp.

Her gun lay somewhere up the slope. Searching for the Jeep, she spotted it right-side-up. Rem stirred, but he seemed to be incoherent.

Up the slope, one of Ammar's men started down toward Rem. He was a stocky man, maneuvering with ease down the slope. Aiming a pistol, he moved cautiously, as though he were approaching a wild grizzly instead of a man. She looked back up toward what she could see of the SUV. Ammar was nowhere in sight, but the second man made his way down the slope behind the first, making his own path closer to Haley. In fact, he was headed straight for her.

She crawled to where she thought her gun had fallen.

The first man was too intent on Rem to notice, and thick vegetation gave her good cover. She crept like a sniper, spotting her gun. She stopped breathing as the man neared the Jeep. He was going to kill Rem.

Rem moved his head more. He seemed to be snapping out of whatever bang to his head he'd suffered.

Haley slid her hand around the grip of her pistol. Raised it. The man peered into the Jeep. He was looking for the diamonds. But then he looked up and spotted her. Seeing him begin to swing his aim toward her, she fired. At last, Rem came to life. He climbed clumsily out of the Jeep, falling to the ground and disappearing from her view. The man closer to her began firing. She stayed low on the ground.

Rem straightened with a gun in his hand and started firing back at the second man, who found cover behind a tree. Rem's gun clicked empty. His target eased out from behind the tree and fired. Haley fired to cover Rem and he ducked out of sight again. She checked above him on the road. She couldn't see the SUV, nor could she see Ammar.

Rem made his way around the Jeep, using it for protection as the man higher up on the slope fired at him. Two clicks signified when his gun was empty. Rem needed no more invitation. He bolted up the hill after him. The other man turned and tried to run to the SUV.

Haley climbed toward the road, wanting to see where Ammar had gone.

Rem and the other man clashed into a roll, fighting on the damp, leafy ground. She climbed faster, aiming her pistol, but was unable to get a clear shot through the trees. Rem overpowered the man, straddling him and punching his face.

Someone grabbed her arm and pulled. She stumbled and almost lost her balance. The hand squeezed her wrist so hard she yelped, then banged her hand against a tree truck until she dropped her pistol. A strong arm hooked her by the waist. Haley arched her neck enough to see it was Ammar who held her. He pressed a gun to her temple.

Haley frantically tried to strategize how to free herself. Rem finished off the other man and pulled a pistol from somewhere on the motionless body. Standing, he turned to face her and Ammar, a pistol hanging from his right hand.

"Drop your weapon or I will shoot her," Ammar called through the trees.

Rem didn't move.

Haley bent her arm and rammed her elbow backward. Feeling the gun leave contact with her temple, she dropped her weight.

Hearing Rem fire his pistol, she didn't have to look to know Ammar was dead before his body thumped to the ground behind her.

After Rem found them a hotel room, he left to case the perimeter, to look for anything suspicious and make sure they hadn't been followed. Alone for a few minutes, Haley called Cullen on the satellite phone. It was no small comfort to know backup was on the way. Odie had promised to take care of everything.

Moments after she disconnected the call, Rem entered the sparse but clean room. He put his gun down and removed his shirt, letting it fall to the floor. His fleeting grimace and traces of blood on his temple cooled her notice of bare skin and muscle. He went into the bathroom and, looking in the mirror, began parting his hair.

Haley found a small first-aid kit in Rem's duffel and followed him into the bathroom. He had the faucet running and was washing his head, turning the cloth and water red.

"Do you need stitches?" she asked.

"No."

She doubted he'd get them even if he did. Taking out a razor and a roll of thin white tape, she reached up and took the cloth from him. Putting her hand on his thick, hard shoulder, she urged him to face her. He did.

Those ice-blue eyes watched her, their intensity riveting. She met them a moment, feeling a bit of reckless fascination when heat flickered to warm life there as she continued to stare.

"Sit on the toilet." The command came with a sultry tone.

He backed up and sat next to the sink. She moved between his parted knees and brushed some hair aside to see his wound.

"Not too bad," she said. "You have a good lump, but the cut isn't very long. I think a couple strips of tape should do." She looked down at him. "I'll need to shave a little hair."

She found a miniature scissors in the first-aid kit and carefully cut the hair around the wound. He had thick enough hair that no one would know he had a cut there.

Using the razor, she shaved around the cut. It was a patchy job, but at least the tape would stick. She dabbed the wound with some dry gauze and applied ointment before making a cross with the tape.

"There." She smoothed his hair over her work.

Looking down, she watched his eyes lift. She angled her head in mock reproach, a silent admonishment for where he'd been ogling.

A grin hitched higher to the left side of his mouth, adding humor to the heat in his impossibly light eyes. It caused a flutter down low that spread to her limbs. And a warning went off in her head. Any more of this and she'd fall too hard for him. She stepped back.

"I need a shower," she said. Anything to get away from him right now.

His eyes smoldered with her unintended invitation. He came to his feet and moved toward her. She put her hand on his chest.

"Alone." She smiled to cover her nervousness.

He chuckled and went around her. "Don't use all the hot water." He closed the door behind him.

While she undressed, she imagined him on the other side of the door. There was something erotic about being naked with only a door separating her from a man who'd already sent her body to the stars. What would happen if he made love to her again? Without Iraq in the way? It worried her.

She turned on the shower, then climbed in when it was hot. Why him? Why did it have to be him that did that for her? She'd wondered it before, many times, and still she had no answer. It baffled her. She wished she could understand what it was about him that worked, and why someone like Travis didn't.

She showered quickly, not because she was afraid the hot water would run out. She didn't want her meandering thoughts that bordered on fantasy to chisel down her defenses. A man like Rem might work for her on a baser level, but she needed someone less larger-than-life for the long term. Rem might force the demons from her soul, but could he have and hold what was left when they were gone?

After drying off, she dressed in a long, sleeveless T-shirt and left the bathroom. Rem stood from a chair. He'd turned on the TV.

The room had two beds, so she picked one and climbed in. The sound of the shower running had her thinking of Rem in there. Soft, wet flesh over hard muscle. Kissing his mouth under the spray of water.

The shower shut off.

Haley's heart jumped. He would come out now. She could take off her T-shirt nightie and be naked when he saw her....

Oh. That idea sent heat swirling.

To have him see her like that…

The bathroom door opened. Rem came out, holding a towel around his sexy, trim hips. Haley swallowed. He stopped when he saw her. She met his gaze for a few sizzling moments, feeling sparks scatter and burst all the way to her core.

Without moving his eyes from her, he went to his duffel and bent to retrieve a pair of jeans. Straightening, he stood still, jeans in one hand, the other holding the towel. She wondered if he was contemplating acting on the desire in her eyes.

But at last he turned and disappeared inside the bathroom.

Haley breathed a few deliberate breaths. What was the matter with her? Did she really want to risk exploring where this led? Did she want to put her heart out that far for him?

She looked at the closed bathroom door. It would be a mistake.

Or would it?

Did she know him better than she gave herself credit for? Could she make him see what she saw in him? What if it was too late for that? What if he refused to accept her on his level? Did it matter? Maybe she didn't need Rem after they got home. Maybe all she needed was this sexual encounter. Instead of trying to predict the future, she should stay right here in the now. And the now consumed her with want. She wanted him. Nothing in her gut told her it was wrong.

Tossing the covers off her feet, she wiggled the hem of the T-shirt out from under her butt and pulled it over her head. She heard the bathroom door open. Still holding the T-shirt in her hands, she hesitated as her gaze locked with Rem's. He froze in the doorway of the bathroom. Wearing only jeans, he was sexier than any other man she'd ever seen.

She held the T-shirt in one hand and extended her arm to let it drop to the floor beside the bed.

Rem's jaw flexed and his eyes hardened.

Bolstering her nerve, she leaned back on her hands, straightening her back to push her breasts up along the arch of her body. Nothing covered her. Her legs were long and slender on the sheets. She knew she was fit. She didn't think she had a model's beauty, nor did she want it. Better to be her own, natural self.

Amazing, how she wanted to show Rem that now. And so unabashedly. Without fear. It was an exhilarating feeling. She let it fuel her passion.

His gaze roamed up her legs, over her pelvis, her breasts, and finally to her face. She understood his silent message. With a slight lift to one corner of his mouth, his head dipped forward just a fraction, changing his eyes, making them gleam with certainty. The certainty of what he intended to do.

Walking to the foot of the bed, he looked at her again. Haley felt his gaze as if it physically caressed her. She watched his ice-blue eyes go from her eyes, to her mouth, down the column of her neck, to her breasts. Further, over her ribs to her slender waist.

When those eyes she was beginning to know so well reached the part of her that yearned for him, she lay back on the bed, folding her arms above her head, sliding her feet up the mattress to bend her knees and part them.

Hunger flared in his eyes and in the set of his mouth. His biceps bulged as he bent his arms to unfasten his jeans. He slid them down his legs and kicked them aside.

Rather than crawl on top of her, he stood before her, allowing her the same liberty she'd offered him. She smiled with the surge of answering pleasure the gesture gave her. She looked her fill. From shoulders to chest, over to biceps and down to a fit, rippling stomach, she took it all in.

Lifting her gaze, she met Rem's and waited for him to make his move. He didn't take long. He put one knee on the mattress and then the other, straddling her. The intensity of his nearness, his presence, his big form tall and looming above her rocked her.

He didn't move, just continued to look down at her, but only her face now. All that delicious, hot, lusciously incandescent intensity surrounded her, a man at odds with the heroism that burned alive and well in his soul. The knowledge of its existence flowered her entire body with glorious sensation. That was what she loved about him. The core of him that even he didn't recognize.

Loved.

Not that. She struggled with the thought.

Rem seemed to sense the change in her and lowered to press his warm, soft mouth against hers. It sent fire curling through her. He moved his knees between her legs, fanning the flames hotter. Her hesitation burned to ashes. This man was hers. Maybe not forever, but he was hers for now. This night. These precious moments of intimacy.

And that was all she needed.

He leaned over her, bracing his weight on one hand while the other spread a path of fire over her hip and indent of her waist. His entire hand, palm and fingers, curved from her ribs to her back as he ran it up her body. His palm caught on the delicate skin of her breast and paused. He cupped her, ran his thumb over her nipple, before sliding back down her body.

Haley tipped her head back against the mattress with the riptide of sensation that coursed through her.

He spread her legs wider with his knees. Her heart drummed thicker and heavier. He slid his hand down her thigh. Back up again. Took gentle hold of one butt cheek. Kissed her. He moved his mouth over hers as though reveling in her sweet acquiescence. Tingles assuaged her skin, shooting from where he kissed her, where his hand kneaded her butt, swirling in her core, numbing the very tips of her limbs. She felt him everywhere.

When his tongue swept deep into her mouth, artfully dancing, circling slowly with hers, she couldn't stop a soft moan.

A harsher sound answered her and he abandoned her mouth to trail breathy kisses from her jaw down the column of her neck. Too soon, he withdrew. Rolling onto his back, he pushed himself up so that he leaned against the ornate, dark wood headboard. He looked messy and masculine against the backdrop.

When he extended his right hand, across his body and toward her, she understood what he wanted. Her. On top of him. While he sat upright, leaning against the headboard.

Shards of heat gave her an intimate throb between her legs. How did he know?

She didn't need an answer. He knew her history. With her on top, she'd be in control and it would have no resemblance to Iraq. She wanted to tell him it didn't matter anymore. That he'd already chased the demons away. This was for her now, her first intimate experience without fear. He'd given that to her.

Moisture stung her eyes. She bit her lower lip to keep the sob climbing up her throat from ruining this moment. But he saw her reaction anyway, and his eyes softened, another dichotomy to a man whose past defined him too harshly.

Haley swallowed the surging emotion in her and crawled over him, straddling his hips. He put his big hands on her hips, and the contact fueled the escalating warmth flowing through every nerve ending in her body.

She touched his chest, looking at her hands because looking at his face was too overwhelming. She caressed his pectorals, marveling at the softness over hard muscle underneath. Feeling him watch her, very aware of his unmoving hands on her hips, she couldn't meet his eyes. Instead, she gave all her attention to touching him. She ran her hands down his body, spending time on his stomach. Fascination made her breathe faster. He had a fine covering of hair that tapered to a barely noticeable line leading to his groin.

The sight of her sitting on him deepened the ache between her legs. She felt his erection between her spread thighs.

Running her hands back up his body, she found leverage on his shoulders and moved her hips to drag herself up his length.

"Uh," she heard him grunt.

She closed her eyes and dragged herself down, up again, down, pressing harder.

He leaned his head back against the headboard and shut his eyes.

His struggle for control made her smile. She planted her mouth on his.

He immediately took over the kiss, cupping the back of her head and lifting his head off the headboard to drive his tongue deep into her mouth.

As she continued to move, his hands tightened on her waist, as though he meant to stop her, but then he let her go. His head thumped against the headboard, and he breathed deep and heavy as his hungry eyes watched her.

"Woman, you're going to kill me," he rasped.

"Shhh," she whispered against his mouth.

He chuckled deeply.

She kissed the column of his neck. The ridge of his jaw. Along his cheek, until she slowed and hovered over his mouth.

Looking into his eyes, she waited, not touching him. He looked back at her, those powerful, ice-blue eyes full of manly desire. It almost pushed her over her threshold of restraint.

She wanted to crush her mouth to his but withheld, wanting him to take the initiative, to feel the strength of desire driving him, to know it was her he wanted so fiercely.

Opening his mouth, he closed his lips over hers, a sensual mating, angling his head and deepening the play of movement. Endless seconds passed before she felt his tongue seek permission for more. She didn't give it to him. Lifting her mouth, she hovered again.

But she didn't have the upper hand for long. With his hand once again on the back of her head, he pulled her against his mouth and had his way with her, taking her with tender, intimate force. Initiative was not something he lacked. She should have known he wouldn't disappoint.

Reestablishing her seat on his erection, she put her hands on his chest. He leaned against the headboard again, dropping his hands to the mattress.

The knowledge that he would wait for her, that he was being so very patient with her, drenched her with love that clamored for release. Rising up onto her knees, she was about to lower her hand to guide him when he did it for her. Sliding one hand up her bare thigh, he held his erection with the other and put the tip of it against her wetness.

Haley let her weight work for her, moving when she needed to until the tip of him parted her. She used her weight to take him deeper, going slowly, allowing her flesh time to stretch for him. When she could take no more of him, she leaned forward, folding her arms around his neck, kissing him. Her nipples brushed his chest before she pressed them flush against him.

His hands moved up her back, then back down, his palms curving over each butt cheek, kneading, spreading, while grinding her where she needed it most. The pressure of his hardness, the friction of it, stimulated her beyond comprehension. She lifted a little, then sank back down. Her movement aided his practiced hands. Feeling an incredible orgasm build, she crushed her mouth onto his and he kissed her masterfully while she came, the play of his tongue adding to the electrifying stroke of their flesh.

"Rem," she whispered, as her orgasm peaked. She loved him. Loved him. Loved him.

His guttural moan followed.

She collapsed against him, only then hearing the way their breathing filled the room.

"Oh, God." The chant of words still echoed in her head. "I think I really am in love with you."

His breathing stopped abruptly.

She tensed. Her thighs, her arms, her back. Her entire body went still.

It was just the sex, right? She couldn't remember it ever being so spectacular before Iraq. Maybe that was why. Her newfound freedom was explosive. Poignant. It couldn't be love.

A feeling in her gut contradicted her desperately careening thoughts.

His hands ran up her arms to her biceps, where he gently held her and moved her back. She almost couldn't look at his face. But the growing realization that what she felt was real froze her.

He searched her eyes with his.

How could she love him?

She felt her brow tighten along with her confusion. *Him?* How could she love *him?*

"Do you?" he asked.

And she saw that he genuinely wanted to know.

"I…"

"Haley—"

"Rem, I…I—I…" She couldn't finish. What could she say except…yes…?

Tears blurred her vision. What did it mean for her? Would he love her back? Did she want him to? Would he be able to give her any kind of future? She didn't think so. Maybe a few months of this…hot, sweaty sex that made her shake and quiver and lose awareness of anything else. But…she loved him.

"Why did it have to be you?" She shook her head. "Why you?" She didn't understand. She didn't think she ever would.

His eyes changed, going from searching and hopeful...yes, hopeful...to something that pinched her heart. Did he want her to love him?

She didn't have time to assimilate something to say. He lifted her off him, depositing her onto the bed beside him. Without pausing, he propelled himself off the bed and started yanking on his jeans.

"Rem, I—"

"Save it, Haley," he hissed. "We both know what this is really all about."

"What?"

"You don't belong here. You never did."

"No, it's not that, it's—"

"Don't say it, Haley."

"Wwwhha—"

He bent over her, fierce and angry, putting his hands on the bed, bracketing her with his arms. "You don't belong with me."

So, he finally said what she'd suspected all along. She rolled her head from side to side, telling him what she couldn't find words to explain.

"I'm not Cullen," he said in a raspy, deep voice. God, she would never get tired of listening to his voice.

"You're not unlike him, either," she finally said. Her delay sent him the wrong message.

He pushed off the bed and straightened. The anger on his face, the hurt emotion, wrenched her. He was misinterpreting her meaning and she didn't know how to tell him what she felt. Not without hurting him more. She didn't want to hurt him.

He threw on a shirt and sat on the bed to put on shoes.

Haley went to him, sitting on her knees and putting her hands on his back. "Rem, don't go."

He stood and turned. She dropped her hands to the mattress.

"I can't stay here with you right now." His gaze lowered and took in her nudity. "Not like this. Not after…"

"Rem…" What could she say? That she meant what she said—that she loved him? That she didn't want to? It was all true, but it wouldn't make him feel better. She didn't trust him to open his heart to her, to overcome his past enough to do that.

His jaw flexed as he continued to misinterpret her feelings. He thought she regretted loving him because she couldn't accept him as he was.

"You're a good man, Rem," she said.

But his face only darkened. "Just not good enough, huh?"

She felt his anger vibrating at her from across the room. Seconds passed as he met her eyes. She tried to plead with him to understand in the silence hanging between them. But it was no use.

He started for the door.

"Rem, please don't go." Where would he go and how long would he be gone? Would he ever come back?

He didn't even glance at her or pause, just opened the door and slammed it on his way out.

She slumped back on the bed and stared at the ceiling. What would have happened had she not said what she had? If she'd only have kept her feelings to herself. Rode them out to see where they led, maybe she wouldn't have hurt him.

Sighing, she rolled her head to the side and looked across the mattress, so empty now without him there. The memory of him beneath her swept her, taking her breath and awing her. She never would have dreamed it possible. That a man would make her feel the way Rem had.

She closed her eyes and let the last hour replay in her imagination, feeling him all over again. The sex wouldn't have been so poignant if she didn't feel strongly for him. Whatever chemistry mixed when they were together, its potency had erupted along with her orgasm. For better or worse, she did love him.

Rem D'Evereux. Criminal adolescent grown into a ruthless man. Soft, sweet warmth engulfed her. No, not ruthless. Underneath all that indefatigable armor was the kindest man she'd ever known. The most honorable. Everything he did, all his battles, were driven by it. But as long as he kept feeding that armor, she'd never crack him open. And until she did, there was no hope of any future for them.

Well. Maybe she'd just have to find a way to crack him.

A sound outside the door made her lift her head. Elation jumped inside her. Had he returned so soon?

She climbed off the bed and hastily dressed in shorts and a white, short-sleeved T-shirt. He didn't open the door. Was he hesitating?

Walking to the door, she looked through the peephole. No one was there.

She opened the door and looked down the hall to her left, toward the elevators. No one. Disappointment sank her spirits. She started to go back into the room. But something hard jabbed her ribs.

"Remember where you are," a man's voice said low beside her ear. "I can kill you right now and no one will care."

She moved her eyes to see him. He wasn't very tall, but he was taller than her, and very well built. His dark eyes were cold and empty, his dark hair thick and dirty and uncombed. The stubble on his face had to be at least three days old.

"You will come with me quietly, or I will kill you."

She could probably take him. He was only one man. Going

with him would be her death sentence, but not before she'd relive the horror of Iraq.

She couldn't go with him. No matter what, she had to find a way to get away from him before they left this hotel.

But no one was walking the halls at this hour. She had no choice other than to allow him to walk her toward the stairs. The door to them opened, and to her utter dread, another man appeared, armed and dark like his friend.

Her heart throbbed in tune with her fear. How would she get away now?

Rem.

Where was he?

She searched the visible halls for him, frantic and desperate. The man with the gun at her ribs shoved her and she stumbled into the stairwell.

Chapter 13

The whiskey Rem had downed pooled in his stomach, making him feel nauseous. He came to the room door and paused. He wasn't ready to face her. When she'd said she thought she loved him, he'd felt his heart cave in on itself. Hearing those words from Haley's sweet mouth had reduced him to a weakened man. He couldn't stop the surge of joy and hope. Dare he believe she loved him? That's what had made him ask her. He was too afraid to believe she actually could.

To discover she didn't had crushed him. He didn't know how to handle that, the way it made him feel to know she'd confused great sex with love, if only for a moment. Respect was as important as good sex in a relationship. He and Haley had proved the sex was as good as it gets, but she didn't respect him.

Well, standing out here in the hall like a timid schoolboy wasn't going to solve anything.

Steeling his nerve, bolstering his defenses, he opened the door and stepped inside. The bed was empty. The bathroom door was open and the light was out.

"Haley?" But he knew she wasn't in the room. It wasn't big enough for her to hide.

Apprehension soured his stomach further. Damn it. He shouldn't have left her alone. Had she left for good?

A quick search around the room confirmed she hadn't packed or taken anything with her. Not even her gun.

Apprehension mushroomed into all-out fear. Where had she gone?

The room door showed no signs of forced entry. So she must have left on her own will. But with Farid and his men waiting for the perfect moment to strike?

He hissed a line of curses. He'd let his pride walk him out the door and now she could be in danger. After Iraq, that would not be easy for her to endure.

Oh, God, please let her be somewhere safe. He shoved his gun into the waist of his jeans and left the room. Running down the stairs, he emerged in the lobby and went to the reception counter. No one was there.

"Hello?" he called.

He cursed in silence inside his head. Anyone could have hauled her right through the front door without being noticed.

A skinny Latino man appeared from a back room, yawning.

"Has anyone come through here in the last hour?" he asked, furious.

The man shrugged. "I no see anyone."

Rem slapped the counter with his palms and fought to contain his anger.

"But someone did leave this for a Rem D'Evereux. Are you that man?"

Rem snatched the envelope from the man's bony hand. He tore it open and nearly ripped the paper as he unfolded it.

Only an address was handwritten there. Farid knew he didn't need to write more. He wanted the diamonds. And if Rem didn't bring them, he'd kill Haley.

Crumpling the paper in his fist, he tossed it to the floor and headed for the exit.

A thousand thoughts and emotions assailed him. Memories of his sister. The last time he'd spoken to her. Finding her broken and bloody body in her condo. Learning who'd given the order and who'd really orchestrated the kill. Farid. Ammar. The lies. Dane and his poor choice in clientele had cost him too much.

Ammar had taken great pleasure in deceiving him. Rem was glad he was dead, but Farid was far more dangerous. One slip and it would cost Haley her life.

He climbed into the Jeep. He knew the address Farid had written. It was the ranch where Dane had sent him, the one where he'd thought he was protecting the inhabitants from rebels instead of working a big drug deal.

Rem had looked there months ago, but Farid hadn't been there. He must have returned after he thought it was safe, after he thought the United States had stopped looking for him here. Or thought he wouldn't be stupid enough to hide in plain sight.

An hour or so later, he passed the gate leading to the compound. A guard shack was active tonight. No surprise there.

He'd have to find a place to park this Jeep and hike in. Hang on, Haley…

"I'm coming to get you," he said.

The unkempt dark-haired man gripped Haley's arm so tight that it pinched. She registered as much as she could of the layout of the ranch-style house. Passing through a large, open room with white walls and black furniture, she noted the back patio door and the front entrance. They'd come through the garage. The décor was as cold as its owner. White walls and black furniture accented with black-and-white prints on the walls.

Down a hallway, they passed a bathroom and came to a circular area with four doors. After spending the last hour in the backseat of a Mercedes SUV with deeply tinted windows and a gun sticking against her side, she was beginning to lose hope that she'd find an opportunity to escape.

The dark-haired man's partner opened a door, and the one behind her pushed her inside. She spun to face them just as the dark-haired man shut the door. She heard a lock slide into place.

Haley scanned the room, turning to see it all. There was a bed and a dresser and a bathroom. She moved to the window and yanked the heavy draperies aside. The window was barred. She went to the dresser and opened the drawers. They were empty. The bathroom was devoid of everything but toilet paper.

Rubbing her arms, she wandered back into the room. The silence disturbed her. She struggled with the encroaching familiarity of her situation. Giving in to fear would not help her.

The sound of the deadbolt clicking sent her heart skittering. The door opened and a man wearing a turban and white long-sleeved shirt entered ahead of the dark-skinned man and his toothless partner. An Osama bin Laden look-alike. She subdued a shiver. This had to be Farid.

He walked with the arrogance of a man ruled by his ego. His eyes looked at her with the appraisal of a hog farmer debating an auction bid. Women were of no more value than that to cruel men like him.

"I trust your accommodations are sufficient?" he said, coming to a stop a few feet from her. The dark-skinned man and his toothless partner flanked him.

She knew better than to think he actually cared about her

accommodations. When she didn't answer, he approached. His dead black eyes didn't flinch as he met hers, studying, contemplating.

"Tell me who you work for."

"I'm an independent contractor."

"Who hired you?"

She didn't answer.

"Were you sent to find my son?" he asked. "Me?"

"No."

"Why were you in Monrovia?"

"My interest was with Habib Maalouf."

"And Rem D'Evereux? How do you know him?"

"He was watching Habib, too."

"He was watching my son." His voice rose in anger. "And now my son is dead."

She carefully remained silent.

"How well do you know him?"

Why was he asking such a question? He must have recognized her confusion because a slight smile curved the corners of his mouth.

"Not well enough, it would seem," he said.

"I know him enough to know he didn't deserve to lose his sister the way he did."

"What has he told you about that? He killed my cousin? Stopped a drug deal between Dane Charter and my son?" He chuckled. "It's true, for the most part, but I am sure he left out the most important details."

"What are you talking about?"

"Dane Charter stole the drugs from Ammar, and Rem took them from Dane. They did not see things equally, you see. Rem knew that Ammar would pay him handsomely for the return of his drugs and was only too eager to oblige."

"Impossible. Ammar killed his sister. Why would Rem want anything from him but his life?"

"Ammar did not kill his sister. Dane did."

Haley had to subdue the need to sharply inhale. It couldn't be true.

"Ah." Farid nodded with a sickly smile. "So, Rem did not tell you everything."

"What wouldn't he want to tell me?" She tried to appear unaffected, but really she dreaded what he was about to reveal.

"Rem doesn't want anyone to know his association with me and my son. It's the real reason he wants us both dead. Your government is investigating him. They suspect his connection to us. He has everyone fooled into believing it was Ammar who killed his sister, probably to point the finger of guilt away from him."

"You're lying." Odie would have known about the investigation. "Ammar killed Rem's sister." He was too emotional over it for it not to be true. He had a powerful thirst for revenge, and it was focused on Farid and Ammar, not Dane. But Dane was dead….

Farid said nothing.

"Why did Ammar kill Dane?" she asked.

"It was what Rem requested in exchange for the return of the drugs."

Rem wanted someone else to kill his sister's murderer?

Something was strange about Farid's story. "What about your cousin?"

"My cousin is another matter. Rem could have made amends for his interference had he done all I asked of him."

"You wanted more from him?"

"He could have worked off his debt to me. When he refused, I threatened to reveal the truth about him to the right people. That is when he began his campaign against me. Had he not taken my diamonds, this would all be over by now. Rem would be dead, and my diamonds on their way to Antwerp." He sighed. "But as I said, that is a separate issue."

If Farid's claim about the drugs were true, Rem had completed a drug deal with terrorists, but he'd done it to get his sister's murderer killed. She didn't know what to think about that. Rem had discovered Dane was dealing drugs and intervened. That intervention had gotten his sister killed. But one thing didn't add up. Instead of completing a drug deal for terrorists, why hadn't he just killed Dane himself? Money? Or was there something else? Something Farid wasn't saying?

"He wouldn't have done it without a good reason," she said.

"Done what? Give me back my drugs? What reason would he need? I paid him a lot of money. Ammar took care of everything."

She could only stare at him while questions popped in her head. She didn't want to believe that she had been so wrong about Rem. Was there something she was missing? Could she afford to hope?

Farid's mouth curved into a wicked grin. "I am pleased you did not know this until now. You've captured his heart and that will serve me well. When he comes for you, I will kill him."

"Then you'll never find your diamonds."

Farid chuckled. "If he does not bring me my diamonds, then it will be you who will die. Your misguided infidel will not let that happen. He will bring me the diamonds." His contemptuous gaze took in her body from her thighs to her breasts. "His weakness for you will ensure this."

It was true. Not the weakness part, but Rem would come for her, and Farid intended to use that to his favor. Rem would know he was running into a trap, but he would come anyway. One man against many. He'd never make it. He'd be killed before he got anywhere near her. And Cullen's team wouldn't make it in time to help.

She tried to keep her breathing steady, but anxiety made it difficult. Rem would be killed and she would be left at the mercy of these men. The similarities to Iraq swarmed her.

She had to get out of here.

Stepping back, she looked at the other two men. They stood on each side of the open door.

Without second-guessing it, she bolted. She made it to the door before one of them grabbed her arm. She yanked it free and ran into the hall. Someone gripped a handful of her hair. The force of the pull sent her flying backward. She lost her balance and fell.

The dark-skinned man hauled her to her feet and bent her arm high behind her back, making her grimace. She stumbled back into the room as he pushed her. The toothless man stopped in the doorway, blocking any escape.

The dark-skinned man pushed her again and she landed against Farid. Anger crowded his brow. He pushed her back a step and slapped her. Her head turned to one side. She ignored the sting and swung her hand, catching him by surprise when she hit him back.

His eyes widened before his anger grew stormy, the crease above his long nose deepening, his mouth pressing tighter. He raised a fisted hand and swung to hit her. She blocked the attempt with her arm and slammed the palm of her hand against his ugly nose. Blood sprouted there.

He shouted something in his language. The dark-skinned man and his toothless partner were beside her in an instant, taking hold of her arms. She wrestled to be free of their grasps as images from her time in captivity slammed her. Farid hit her, punched her face so hard she saw white spots dotting her vision. Like when the Iraqi men hit her with their rifles. If the dark-skinned man and his partner weren't holding her, she would have toppled over.

Farid hit her midsection next. She couldn't breathe. He slapped her face.

Ripping clothes. The air on her bare skin. Two men looming. One of them reaching for her pants. Her kick. The rifle smashing against her head.

Breathing through the haze of apprehension, memory mixing with the sight of Farid as he leaned close.

"I do not need you alive for Rem to come for you," he growled.

She stared at his hateful face.

"Do not try my patience."

Recovering from the memories threatening to come into full light, she spat in his face. "You're going to kill me anyway, so why don't you just do it now?"

He wiped dripping blood from his nose. "Do not be so eager to bring about your demise. You tempt me to do as you ask."

With a long, penetrating stare, he moved around her and left the room. The other two men left after him and the deadbolt slid into place, leaving her in silence once again.

Farid wasn't going to kill her until he had Rem. Did that mean he wasn't sure he could? Did he wonder if Rem might succeed in freeing her? Had he been certain, he would have killed her already.

She hoped Farid was right. She hoped Rem would succeed in freeing her. Moving to a chair beside the single bed, she sat there and fought the memories. When they kept coming, she lowered her head into the palms of her hands.

Rem slammed his gun into the back of the guard's head. The guard slumped to the ground, unconscious. Rem looked up one direction along the iron fence to the other. No one moved through the darkness. He figured he had about fifteen minutes before the guard patrolling the perimeter fence would be missed.

Running across the grounds toward the sprawling ranch house, he searched for movement. He saw none as he reached the side of the house. Raising his gun, he stepped sideways along the building. He peered into a darkened window. The blinds were closed. Making it to the corner, he continued down the side of the house, using the shrubbery as cover as he reached the back. Trees and plants surrounded a curving pool. Lights illuminated the water and patio. An armed guard strolled across the stone, looking across the pool and scanning the grounds. Rem ducked behind a shrub as his gaze reached him. He peeked out a few seconds later.

The guard had turned his back and headed the other direction on the patio. Rem slid a knife from the holster strapped to his calf under the hem of his pant leg. Rushing to the back of the man, he made quick work of slicing his throat. Pulling the body into the shadows, Rem leaned his back against the wall beside the sliding glass door.

After a careful glance through the glass, he pushed the door open just enough to slip through. Closing the door again, he moved quietly through a tiled sitting area.

He didn't hear any sounds. Quiet was good. Hearing Haley scream would probably bring him to his knees.

Taking a couple of deep breaths, he proceeded forward. A hallway opened to two doors that he could see. There were probably more.

Muffled voices reached him. Now he heard the elevated sound of a female's voice, hissing something he couldn't decipher. It was quickly followed by a crash.

Rem ran.

At the door, he checked the knob. Unlocked. He turned it and then pushed it open with his foot. As the door banged against the adjacent wall, he charged in, ready to fire at anything that wasn't Haley. He saw her in his peripheral vision, struggling with a dark-haired man. He swung her around, using her as a shield.

Another man appeared to his left. Rem swung his weapon the same instant the other man fired his own. The bullet grazed his arm. He felt it slice through the material of his shirt. It didn't matter. The man was dead now, a hole in his forehead from Rem's bullet.

Rem faced Haley and her struggle with the dark-haired man. He stepped closer, watching her free herself from the man's grip and turn toward him. She blocked his fist and knocked his gun from his hand.

Rem fired his own gun. The man collapsed forward, pushing Haley off balance. But she quickly regained it and jumped out of the way as the man's body fell to the floor.

Rem stepped before her and cupped her chin in his hand and kissed her quick and hard.

"Rem," she whispered fervently, sending emotion spreading from his brain like shards of wild electricity. She threw her arms around him for a hug.

"We have to get out of here," he said, gently pushing her back.

She removed her arms from him and nodded.

Taking her hand, he led her out of the room and down the hall. No one intercepted them in the house. Rem led Haley outside. Two men emerged from the cover of shrubs on each side of the sliding glass door. He stopped and took as many steps backward as he dared, hoping to get Haley in a position to take cover inside.

Another man appeared, striding toward them slowly. Rem saw the smile on Farid's face and felt rage swell and churn in him.

He almost reacted defensively when he felt Haley's slender hand pull the extra pistol from the back of his pants. It made his resulting smile a lot different than Farid's. She stuck the gun under his left arm.

Enough of a hint for him. He went for the guy on the right and let her take Farid. She fired at the same time. Rem watched the man who caused the gruesome death of his sister slump to the concrete floor of the patio and felt…nothing.

After everything, he'd at least expect to feel relief, maybe even satisfaction. But nothing resembling those emotions rose in him. It was like another job. And it was over.

Something about Haley's behavior was bothering him. After arranging travel to Buenos Aires, Rem had gotten them out of South America, but in all that time, she'd barely spoken to him. And her body language seemed stiffer than usual.

"Are you sure you're all right?" he asked. He'd asked her a couple of times before now, too, and the answer was always the same.

She turned from looking out the darkened plane window as they taxied toward their gate. "Yes."

It was too blasé. Just like the other times he'd asked.

"You don't seem to be."

"I'm fine."

"Did something happen at Farid's ranch? Did any of them hurt you?"

"No, not the way you're thinking."

"What's wrong then?"

He could see her hesitation. She didn't want to tell him. Foreboding crept through him.

"I remember," she said.

It took him by surprise. He felt his brain catch up. And then he understood.

She remembered Iraq.

"Haley…" He didn't want her to torment herself with reliving it more than she already had.

"No," she stopped him. "It's okay."

He studied her. In her eyes he saw she meant it. In fact, she seemed more than okay with it. Which only convinced him that something else was wrong. Something else had made her withdraw into her thoughts. What he wanted to know was why she wasn't saying anything about it. Because he had a feeling it was about him.

"After we were attacked," she began, "after everyone else was killed except me, there were three Iraqis left."

"One was angrier than the others." Now she got a faraway look in her eyes and he knew she wasn't as unaffected as he thought. "He used his AK-47 to beat me. I fought him. And I managed to loosen the weapon from his hands. I turned it on him and shot." She paused. "I killed him, but that angered his friends. The two of them together were too hard to fight. They both beat me, with their guns, with their fists. I couldn't...I just...I couldn't fight them."

"You don't have to tell me," he said, taking her hand.

She only shook her head, telling him she needed this. She needed to say it.

He clamped down on his protective instincts and let her go on.

"I...remember them ripping my clothes. That was after they hit me many times. My head was so foggy. I was dizzy. And sick to my stomach. And in pain. The pain in my head was excruciating. I was barely aware by then."

Rem forced himself to keep his eyes direct and detached as her remembering eyes found his.

"The last thing I remember is I was topless and one of them held my hands while the other went for the buttons of my pants. I kicked him and he hit me with his rifle."

Rem gritted his teeth.

"That's the last thing I remember," she said.

He knew then that she'd finished.

"Haley." He heard the rasp in his own tone. "I wish I could have been there for you."

She breathed a soft laugh. "I wish that, too. But it's okay now. I'm okay now. It's behind me and I can move on with my life."

"Does that mean you're going to quit TES?"

"No. I'll always fight terrorism. But Cullen and Travis were right. I can do that without ever leaving the States."

Looking at her, seeing the peace on her face, he knew that she had put it behind her. Confirming that she had gone unconscious during the abuse helped. She would never have to relive the worst of it.

He smiled, glad for her. But then he recalled her withdrawal and felt his smile drain away as it dawned on him what must have happened. She'd been held captive by Farid. If he'd spoken with her...

"It isn't true," he said.

She turned her gaze on him.

"Whatever he told you," he added.

"Who?"

"Farid."

"You won't tell me the truth anyway."

"Is that why you didn't say anything?"

"Why bother?"

"So, you believe him." The notion dug into his heart and twisted.

It took her a while to respond. "Why didn't you tell me?"

Exactly as he'd feared. She believed Farid. The confirmation of that swelled into a caldron of emotion. He felt betrayed. By her. And a sinking feeling followed when he realized why. Somewhere along the way, he'd fallen in love with her. Her sweetness had worked its way through him. So had her constant conviction that he was more like Cullen than he thought. But along with that had always been her doubt.

He turned his head, unable to look at her beauty any longer.

She'd been wavering since the beginning. Her heart wanted to believe he was good enough for her, but her mind knew better. Never in his imagination would he have thought he'd ever want to be wrong. That for the first time ever, he regretted the bad decisions of his youth. That he could be the man Haley wanted him to be. He could almost despise her for making him feel that way. Except he couldn't. Because he loved her. He loved her, but he couldn't have her. He'd known that from the start. Why had he let himself forget that? Even for one minute?

"Why?" she asked from beside him.

He met her eyes and couldn't discern what thoughts hovered beyond their deep blue depth. "Because I knew what you'd think."

"Tell me the truth, Rem."

"I already have."

Chapter 14

Haley followed Rem into RC Mountaineering; she hadn't missed that he carried the diamonds. After talking to Cullen without Rem knowing, she more than dreaded this meeting. She'd told her boss about the drugs and what Farid had said. Cullen worried she'd never get out of South America if any of it was true, so he'd told her not to say anything to Rem until they arrived at Headquarters in Roaring Creek.

I already have.

Whatever Farid had told her, it wasn't true. That was what he'd meant on the plane. And Haley believed him. She believed whatever he'd done, he had a good reason that whatever wrong was in it he'd righted. He was too accustomed to people thinking the worst. She didn't know how to show him how wrong he was.

Odie approached from displays of clothes and gear, dark hair bunched in a messy pile on top of her head.

"It's about time you two made it here," she said.

"Odie," Haley greeted.

Odie gave her a brief hug before turning to Rem, unabashedly giving him an observant once-over.

"Rem D'Evereux, Odelia Frank," Haley introduced.

"Well, you brought her back," Odie said. "That's something, anyway."

"Leave them alone, Odie." Cullen emerged from the basement, stopping before he reached the top step, just far enough to see them. He didn't sound or look happy. "Let's go downstairs."

Rem sent her an accusatory look before following. She followed, too, struggling with how to convey she'd never stopped believing him, in him. In a conference room to the right of the stairs, Cullen pulled a chair out for Haley.

"I'll stand," she said.

Cullen turned to Rem, who'd moved to the other side of the long table. Not much else adorned the room. One wall was left blank to hang maps and satellite images, the other had a huge, currently blank whiteboard. The far wall opposite the door had a picture of the Twin Towers under a crystalline blue New York City sky, before 9/11. It was the only picture in the room.

"I had an interesting talk with a friend at the DEA," Cullen began. "Any ideas what might have been the topic?"

Rem smirked. "I'll bet he gave you an earful."

"He confirmed what Haley told me."

That removed any expression from Rem's face, but when he turned his head his eyes were cold. It was like invisible daggers pierced her.

"She wasn't inclined to believe Farid, but in this case, it turns out he was right."

Haley turned from Rem. "Cullen." She silently implored him.

He didn't acknowledge her, but she knew he was aware of her anxiety.

"If it isn't true, why didn't you tell us?" he said to Rem.

"What did your friend tell you?" Rem asked instead of answering.

"They'd like to ask you a few questions, the biggest being why you took cocaine from Dane Charter and sold it to Ammar."

"I never sold anything to Ammar."

"The agent I spoke with said he saw you. Even has pictures." Cullen dropped them on the table. Rem looked down at them and then at Haley.

She could read what he was thinking, wondering what she thought, if she believed all of this. She shook her head. Could he see in her eyes that she trusted him?

But his gaze left hers for Cullen's. "Ammar promised to tell me where I could find Charter in exchange for the drugs. I wanted that more than anything at the time."

"How long did you work with him and his son?" Cullen asked.

"I never worked with them."

"You gave him drugs."

"That was an exception."

"You make pretty loose exceptions, given they were terrorists."

She couldn't take it anymore. "Cullen, stop."

"We need to resolve this, Haley," Cullen said. "Why did you go after them? Why did you want them dead? Seems to me they did you a favor."

Rem just stood there, letting Cullen piece it all together. All the bad news. Why wasn't he defending himself? Why was he letting Cullen think so poorly of him?

"Were you afraid of what they'd reveal to the DEA?" Cullen pressed.

That pulled a change from Rem. Anger radiated from him as he dumped the leather bag onto the conference room table. "I hope you put these to good use." Then without another word, he straightened and went to the conference room door.

"Rem," Haley called.

But he never paused. He just kept going. She let him. Nothing she said right now would sway him anyway. And that made her feel so hopeless. What was she going to do?

"I'm sorry, Haley. I thought he was different."

I already have. He'd already told the truth.

She turned from the empty doorway to look at Cullen. "Farid was lying about Rem's sister."

Cullen gave her a sympathetic frown. "Too much of what he said corroborated with the agent's claims."

"But…what if Farid and Ammar lied to Rem? They wanted their cocaine back. And in the end, they wanted their diamonds back, too. Wouldn't they try anything? *Say* anything?"

She watched Cullen mull that over. "I know you want that to be true, but—"

"No," she cut him off. "Listen to me. It gives Rem a compelling reason to go after them." It explained the depth of his emotion, too, and his relentless drive to taste revenge.

"Whatever happened between him and Ammar, whatever reason he gave Ammar those drugs, it wasn't without a cause," she said.

"Haley—"

"He had a reason."

He stared at her. And finally she watched him relent. "I'll look into it."

Smiling, she pivoted and ran out of the conference room and up the stairs. Past Odie's startled look, she swung the door open and ran into the street, turning, searching. But he was nowhere. He was gone.

She had no cell phone number. She didn't know where he lived. She only knew he had a villa in Monrovia.

Odie walked into the street and stopped at her side.

"You don't want to wind up with a guy like that anyway," she said.

Haley was too consumed with loss to pay too much attention,

looking down the empty street. "You have to help me find him, Odie."

"Why bother? Nothing but heartache from those kind," Odie said. "You can do better."

Haley shook her head. "You have to help me find him."

Odie's silence made her turn and look at her. Being scrutinized by a woman with Odie's bold self-assurance was never a comforting experience.

"You love him?"

"More than I could ever put into words."

"He's going to break your heart." Odie gave her a once-over. "Look at you, he already has. He walked away, Haley. He's gone. G-o-n-e, *gone*. How could you allow yourself to fall for a man like that?"

Something in Odie's tone clued Haley to a deeper emotion, one that this dynamo had done a good job of hiding until now.

"Go find yourself a nice, steady…anal…and boring… engineer," Odie continued, apparently having missed Haley's growing awareness of the change in her. "Boring is good some-times."

Her choice of words and the faltering sass in her tone made Haley even more curious. "What do you have against men like Rem?"

Odie shrugged, a bad attempt to appear nonchalant. "They're always on a mission. And as a result, always walking with their back to a woman."

"Have you ever had a relationship with an operative?"

Odie's chin jerked up a fraction and her expression sort of stiffened. "I've had relationships with a lot of different men."

"Hmm." Haley bit off what she really wanted to say. The one that hurt the most had to have been an operative. "Is that why you're marrying an anal, boring engineer?"

Odie blinked a few times, as though trying to conceal her fracturing effort to hide the turmoil building in her. It was quite a sight. Haley felt like she was watching history unfold. "They don't come with any complicated baggage." She paused as though debating whether to continue. Her vigorous personality overruled. "Other than a nauseating fondness for detail."

Haley laughed. "You aren't getting married, Odie. You might make it to the altar, but you won't get to the 'I Do' part."

Rem stepped into his condo in Taos, New Mexico, unable to shake the lasting knowledge that Haley was no different than anyone else he'd encountered. Just like the rest, she didn't understand him. Just when he'd begun to trust her. It annoyed him that he'd allowed himself to fall for her so hard.

He took two stairs at a time up to his bedroom. A platform bed barely filled the space of the large room, although it was king-size. He had one dresser and nothing on the walls. He hadn't lived there long enough to make it feel like home. Pulling a carry-on-sized luggage from his closet, he put it on the bed and paused.

Looking at his walls again, white, bland and bare, it struck him that he'd never spent much time here. Once he'd found the place in Monrovia, he'd settled right in. But here, in the States, where so much of his childhood haunted him, he'd never opened his heart to risking a life here.

Funny, how easy it had been to risk a life in places like Monrovia. Meeting Haley had melted a little of that armor. He supposed he'd still been too frozen to see it until now. Until she had to go and turn out like all the rest. Or had she? He'd never given her a chance to talk to him when he'd left. Not liking where his thoughts were headed, he began tossing his belongings into the bag, irritation making his movements more forceful than necessary.

This had happened to him before. He'd met women who ran as soon as they figured out he wasn't ordinary, but there was one, six years ago, who'd wormed her way into his heart the way Haley had. But she couldn't handle what he was. What he did. His actions weren't enough. The label said it all. It was the only affirmation she'd needed. Mercenary. He was a merc. She'd never gotten past it and she'd ended up running. Haley would never know how accurate she'd been about the clothes.

She'd also never know that getting over her would hurt a lot more than the one who'd worn the clothes before her. It would take a long time to forget Haley. But some day he would. It's what he always did. He moved on. He did the best he could and he moved forward.

Continuing to pack what little he'd need, he eased his mind off the woman who'd haunt it for God only knew how long. Aside from feeling the loss of Haley, there was the grave news that Cullen had imparted. The DEA. After him. In his wildest desires for revenge, he'd never seen that one coming. But it wasn't surprising. Farid was on the U.S. government's radar. They'd likely been watching Dane Charter and that was how they'd put it all together. Rem should have considered the possibility that he was being watched by someone other than those affiliated with Dane and Ammar.

It hardly mattered now. What did matter was securing his future. He was practiced in that. It was something he was good at. Nothing he'd aspired to, but the talent was there nonetheless.

He'd go back to Monrovia until he figured out what to do. He'd lay low for a while and see what happened. Move if he had to. Haley knew where to find his villa. She might lead the law to him.

Just the thought of her tightened his chest. He hadn't thought he'd gotten so tangled with her. Maybe it wasn't so much the way he felt about her as it was her easy sway to Cullen's side of things. After all her persuasions. Her taunts and comparisons. Why couldn't she accept him the way he was?

Again, the nagging sensation that something was off came over him. What if he was wrong?

Chapter 15

It was different being in Monrovia this time. Haley listened to her bare feet tread lazily over the cool tile floor of Rem's dining area, licking the icy berry flavor of a frozen Popsicle. She'd already taken a swim in his pool and raided his freezer. It was hot today. She felt naked in her bikini, all by herself, but there was a bounce to her slow, leisurely step; she felt more feminine than she'd felt in a long, long time. And more secure. That was the difference. Her future was less of an unknown now.

She knew Rem was here, in Monrovia. Odie had been right. Haley had found his things in his room and the kitchen was newly stocked. There were dishes in the sink. But she was glad he hadn't been here when she'd charmed his guard into letting her in. It gave her time to acclimate. And prepare for facing Rem with his lifelong struggle of living on the wrong side but acting on the right.

The sound of the front door's lock turning jarred her pulse into a gasping rhythm and stilled her at the same time. Rem stepped inside. He saw her and stopped, swinging the door shut as he stared. She couldn't find her voice. It had been almost two weeks since she'd last seen him.

"How did you get in here?" he asked, his tone flat and unwelcoming.

She had to squelch the urge to throw herself against him and plant kisses all over his face. It was so good to see him again. "Your guard let me in."

He didn't say anything else. Didn't ask why she was here, didn't greet her. Not that she expected him to.

"Rem—"

"You wasted your time coming here." He walked toward her, dumping his keys on the dining room table before standing in front of her.

"I know it was Ammar who killed your sister," she blurted.

"Is that what you came here to tell me?"

"Yes. I also came to tell you that I never stopped believing in you."

He smirked at her.

She stepped closer and put her hand on his chest. "I never doubted you, Rem. You didn't give me a chance to tell you that at TES headquarters."

When he moved back, out of her reach, the rejection stabbed her heart. But she wasn't going to back down. "There's just one thing I don't understand."

"What's that? Why I didn't take money from Ammar?"

"No. Why didn't you go after Dane yourself?"

He took in her face for a few seconds, as though trying to gauge where she was headed with this.

"Ammar said he knew where to find him," he finally said.

"That's what you told Cullen and me. But did you find Dane?"

"No."

"What happened?"

"Ammar gave me an address and the name Charter

supposedly took on. But I never found him. I kept looking, and one thing led to another, until I finally discovered he was murdered the night my sister was killed."

"So Ammar lied to you."

"To get his drugs back."

"Which you gave to him." He had to know how bad that looked.

The same anger and resentment she'd seen in him the day he'd left her at TES headquarters radiated in his eyes now.

"Rem, I never stopped believing in you," she repeated, imploring. Somehow she had to make him understand. "I always knew you wouldn't have done what Farid claimed. Not without a good reason. You should know that. You should know by now that I wouldn't believe anything Farid said."

"It's too late, Haley."

"No." Tears burned her eyes. He was going to shut her out.

A stillness came over him. His eyes still fired their wonderful light, but a calmness, a resignation seemed to take over. "It is. Let me show you why." He turned. "Follow me."

She did, her heart beating heavy with dread. He had yet one more surprise in store for her, and she was so afraid it would mean the end of them. For good.

He went into his office and opened the closet door. He glanced at her.

She looked from him to the closet. A safe was on the floor, not concealed, just pushed back in a corner, under the hang of his shirts.

Rem spun the dial with his combination. The door opened. And inside, piles of a cash were plainly visible.

He looked up at her over his shoulder.

"What is that?" she asked.

"Ammar sold the drugs I gave him, but he never got to do anything with the money."

She stared at him as it all fell into place. Rem had given Ammar the drugs in exchange for information. Somehow, he'd stolen the money Ammar had made when he'd sold the drugs. Ammar had never received the money.

"And he couldn't get the money back from you."

Rem shook his head.

"And then you stole the diamonds."

"I would have taken anything from them that would have made them money."

"Rem…" She could think of nothing else to utter. She wiped her cheek.

"It would never work, Haley."

It would. Didn't he see? "I love you," she whispered.

He looked up at her for a timeless moment. Then he turned toward the closet and pulled a briefcase from the top of the safe. Opening it, he started putting the money inside.

He wasn't even going to acknowledge what she'd just said.

"I want you to give it to Cullen and ask him to pass it on to that DEA agent who took pictures of me with Ammar," he said as he worked.

"You can do that yourself."

He finished putting the money into the briefcase and put it by her feet. Then he stood.

"I was wondering how I was going to get the money into the right hands. So I guess it's good you came here."

"Rem, stop this." She moved closer and put both hands on his chest. "Don't let your pride stop you from having what you know you want."

He reached for her wrists. She slid her hands around to his back, not letting him push her away. He put his hands on each of her arms.

"Cullen asked me to tell you he wants to work out a deal between TES and Pioneer Security Consultants," she said.

He seemed wary and didn't say anything.

"He knows the truth as much as I do," she went on.

"The truth, huh?"

"Yes."

"And what truth would that be?"

"You already know. You've always known. You just have a hard time accepting it."

"What. That I'm the next great American hero?" He grunted.

"Yes," she said with a straight face. "Will you agree to it? Will you work with Cullen?"

"Haley…" He started to push her away, but she clamped her fingers together behind his back.

"What are you so afraid of?"

"I'm not afraid."

"What's stopping you, then?"

His lips pressed closed and he just looked down at her. She saw his desire to believe her along with his reticence.

She rose up onto her toes and brought her lips close to his. "Maybe you need some more convincing." She touched his mouth with hers.

His hands on her arms tightened.

"I love you," she whispered. "I do."

She moved back a fraction, just enough to see his eyes.

"What are you going to do about that?" she asked, kissing him again.

"What do you want me to do?"

She heard his breathing come faster and smiled against his mouth. "Tell me you love me, too."

He slid his hands around to her back and pulled her harder against his body. Then he just looked down at her, breathing through his mouth, a storm of wavering passion in his eyes.

"You're the damnedest woman I've ever met."

"Does that mean you see what an ass you've been?"

"Maybe a little." He kissed her.

"Tell me I was right."

His lips curved into a grin as he kissed her more. "You were right."

She didn't think he completely believed it, but he would. Eventually.

Smiling at his stubbornness, she opened her mouth over his and kissed him harder. "Now, tell me you love me."

"I love you," he rasped.

She threw her arms over his shoulders and folded them behind his neck.

"Does this mean you'll marry me?" he asked.

"Anytime, anywhere."

"Good. But I have one condition."

"What." She kissed him again. "Anything."

"You work intel where it's safe."

That was easy. "Agreed. Yes. Where it's safe."

"Where it's safe, Haley."

"Yes, where it's safe." No more putting herself in danger to overcome her weaknesses. And Rem would never have to doubt what anyone thought of him again. She could feel the change in him, the acceptance of a truth that had been inside him all along. A truth that only she could have unleashed.

When he lifted her, she wrapped her legs around him and he carried her toward his bedroom, alive with a love that had conquered the darkness in them both. She wanted to celebrate that love with Rem. Right now. And for the rest of her life.

* * * * *

*Harlequin Intrigue top author Delores Fossen presents
a brand-new series of breathtaking romantic suspense!*
TEXAS MATERNITY: HOSTAGES
*The first installment available May 2010:
THE BABY'S GUARDIAN*

Shaw cursed and hooked his arm around Sabrina.

Despite the urgency that the deadly gunfire created, he tried to be careful with her, and he took the brunt of the fall when he pulled her to the ground. His shoulder hit hard, but he held on tight to his gun so that it wouldn't be jarred from his hand.

Shaw didn't stop there. He crawled over Sabrina, sheltering her pregnant belly with his body, and he came up ready to return fire.

This was obviously a situation he'd wanted to avoid at all cost. He didn't want his baby in the middle of a fight with these armed fugitives, but when they fired that shot, they'd left him no choice. Now, the trick was to get Sabrina safely out of there.

"Get down," someone on the SWAT team yelled from the roof of the adjacent building.

Shaw did. He dropped lower, covering Sabrina as best he could.

There was another shot, but this one came from a rifleman on the SWAT team. Shaw didn't look up, but he heard the sound of glass being blown apart.

The shots continued, all coming from his men, which meant it might be time to try to get Sabrina to better cover. Shaw glanced at the front of the building.

So that Sabrina's pregnant belly wouldn't be smashed against the ground, Shaw eased off her and moved her to a

sitting position so that her back was against the brick wall.
They were close. Too close. And face-to-face.

He found himself staring right into those sea-green eyes.

How will Shaw get Sabrina out?
Follow the daring rescue and the heartbreaking
aftermath in THE BABY'S GUARDIAN
by Delores Fossen,
available May 2010 from Harlequin Intrigue.

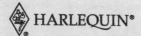

HARLEQUIN®

American ★ Romance®

LAURA MARIE ALTOM

The Baby Twins

Stephanie Olmstead has her hands full raising
her twin baby girls on her own. When she runs
into old friend Brady Flynn, she's shocked to find
herself suddenly attracted to the handsome airline
pilot! Will this flyboy be the perfect daddy—
or will he crash and burn?

Babies
&
Bachelors
USA

"LOVE, HOME & HAPPINESS"

www.eHarlequin.com

HAR75309

HARLEQUIN Presents

Bestselling Harlequin Presents® author

Lynne Graham

introduces

VIRGIN ON HER WEDDING NIGHT

Valente Lorenzatto never forgave Caroline Hales's
abandonment of him at the altar. But now he's
made millions and claimed his aristocratic Venetian
birthright—and he's poised to get his revenge.
He'll ruin Caroline's family by buying out their
company and throwing them out of their mansion...
unless she agrees to give him the wedding night
she denied him five years ago....

**Available May 2010
from Harlequin Presents!**